Harriet B. Stowe

Queer Little People

Harriet B. Stowe

Queer Little People

ISBN/EAN: 9783337325800

Printed in Europe, USA, Canada, Australia, Japan

Cover: Foto ©Andreas Hilbeck / pixelio.de

More available books at **www.hansebooks.com**

Queer Little People.

BY

HARRIET BEECHER STOWE.

Illustrated.

NEW YORK:

FORDS, HOWARD, AND HULBERT.

CONTENTS.

———•———

THE HEN THAT HATCHED DUCKS.

A STORY.

ONCE there was a nice young hen that we will call Mrs.
Feathertop. She was a hen of most excellent family,
being a direct descendant of the Bolton Grays, and as pretty
a young fowl as you should wish to see of a summer's day.
She was, moreover, as fortunately situated in life as it was

possible for a hen to be. She was bought by young Master
Fred Little John, with four or five family connections of
hers, and a lively young cock, who was held to be as brisk
a scratcher and as capable a head of a family as any half-
dozen sensible hens could desire.

I can't say that at first Mrs. Feathertop was a very sensible hen. She was very pretty and lively, to be sure,
and a great favorite with Master Bolton Gray Cock, on
account of her bright eyes, her finely shaded feathers, and
certain saucy dashing ways that she had, which seemed
greatly to take his fancy. But old Mrs. Scratchard, living
in the neighboring yard, assured all the neighborhood that
Gray Cock was a fool for thinking so much of that flighty
young thing, — that she had not the smallest notion how
to get on in life, and thought of nothing in the world but
her own pretty feathers. "Wait till she comes to have
chickens," said Mrs. Scratchard. "Then you will see. I
have brought up ten broods myself, — as likely and respectable chickens as ever were a blessing to society, — and I think
I ought to know a good hatcher and brooder when I see
her; and I know *that* fine piece of trumpery, with her white
feathers tipped with gray, never will come down to family
life. *She* scratch for chickens! Bless me, she never did
anything in all her days but run round and eat the worms
which somebody else scratched up for her.

When Master Bolton Gray heard this he crowed very

loudly, like a cock of spirit, and declared that old Mrs. Scratchard was envious, because she had lost all her own tail-feathers, and looked more like a worn-out old feather-duster than a respectable hen, and that therefore she was filled with sheer envy of anybody that was young and pretty. So young Mrs. Feathertop cackled gay defiance at her busy rubbishy neighbor, as she sunned herself under the bushes on fine June afternoons.

Now Master Fred Little John had been allowed to have these hens by his mamma on the condition that he would build their house himself, and take all the care of it ; and, to do Master Fred justice, he executed the job in a small way quite creditably. He chose a sunny sloping bank covered with a thick growth of bushes, and erected there a nice little hen-house, with two glass windows, a little door, and a good pole for his family to roost on. He made, moreover, a row of nice little boxes with hay in them for nests, and he bought three or four little smooth white china eggs to put in them, so that, when his hens *did* lay, he might carry off their eggs without their being missed. This hen-house stood in a little grove that sloped down to a wide river, just where there was a little cove which reached almost to the hen-house.

This situation inspired one of Master Fred's boy advisers with a new scheme in relation to his poultry enterprise. "Hullo! I say, Fred," said Tom Seymour, "you ought to raise ducks — you 've got a capital place for ducks there."

"Yes, — but I 've bought *hens*, you see," said Freddy; "so it 's no use trying."

"No use! Of course there is! Just as if your hens could n't hatch ducks' eggs. Now you just wait till one of your hens wants to set, and you put ducks' eggs under her, and you 'll have a family of ducks in a twinkling. You can buy ducks' eggs, a plenty, of old Sam under the hill; he always has hens hatch his ducks."

So Freddy thought it would be a good experiment, and informed his mother the next morning that he intended to furnish the ducks for the next Christmas dinner; and when she wondered how he was to come by them, he said, mysteriously, "O, I will show you how!" but did not further explain himself. The next day he went with Tom Seymour, and made a trade with old Sam, and gave him a middle-aged jack-knife for eight of his ducks' eggs. Sam, by the by, was a woolly-headed old negro man, who lived by the pond hard by, and who had long cast envying eyes on Fred's jack-knife, because it was of extra-fine steel, having been a Christmas present the year before. But Fred knew very well there were any number more of jack-knives where that came from, and that, in order to get a new one, he must dispose of the old; so he made the trade and came home rejoicing.

Now about this time Mrs. Feathertop, having laid her eggs daily with great credit to herself, notwithstanding Mrs.

Scratchard's predictions, began to find herself suddenly attacked with nervous symptoms. She lost her gay spirits,
grew dumpish and morose, stuck up her feathers in a bristling way, and pecked at her neighbors if they did so much
as look at her. Master Gray Cock was greatly concerned,
and went to old Doctor Peppercorn, who looked solemn, and
recommended an infusion of angle-worms, and said he would
look in on the patient twice a day till she was better.

"Gracious me, Gray Cock!" said old Goody Kertarkut,
who had been lolling at the corner as he passed, "a'n't you
a fool?— cocks always are fools. Don't you know what's
the matter with your wife? She wants to set,—that's all;
and you just let her set! A fiddlestick for Doctor Peppercorn! Why, any good old hen that has brought up a family
knows more than a doctor about such things. You just go
home and tell her to set, if she wants to, and behave herself."

When Gray Cock came home, he found that Master Freddy
had been before him, and established Mrs. Feathertop upon
eight nice eggs, where she was sitting in gloomy grandeur.
He tried to make a little affable conversation with her, and
to relate his interview with the doctor and Goody Kertarkut, but she was morose and sullen, and only pecked at
him now and then in a very sharp, unpleasant way; so
after a few more efforts to make himself agreeable, he left
her, and went out promenading with the captivating Mrs.

Red Comb, a charming young Spanish widow, who had just been imported into the neighboring yard.

"Bless my soul!" said he, "you've no idea how cross my wife is."

"O you horrid creature!" said Mrs. Red Comb; "how little you feel for the weaknesses of us poor hens!"

"On my word, ma'am," said Gray Cock, "you do me injustice. But when a hen gives way to temper, ma'am, and no longer meets her husband with a smile, — when she even pecks at him whom she is bound to honor and obey —"

"Horrid monster! talking of obedience! I should say, sir, you came straight from Turkey!" and Mrs. Red Comb tossed her head with a most bewitching air, and pretended to run away, and old Mrs. Scratchard looked out of her coop and called to Goody Kertarkut, —

"Look how Mr. Gray Cock is flirting with that widow. I always knew she was a baggage."

"And his poor wife left at home alone," said Goody Kertarkut. "It's the way with 'em all!"

"Yes, yes," said Dame Scratchard, "she'll know what real life is now, and she won't go about holding her head so high, and looking down on her practical neighbors that have raised families."

"Poor thing, what'll she do with a family?" said Goody Kertarkut.

"Well, what business have such young flirts to get mar-

ried?" said Dame Scratchard. "I don't expect she 'll raise
a single chick; and there 's Gray Cock flirting about, fine
as ever. Folks did n't do so when I was young. I 'm sure
my husband knew what treatment a setting hen ought to
have, — poor old Long Spur, — he never minded a peck or
so now and then I must say these modern fowls a'n't what
fowls used to be."

Meanwhile the sun rose and set, and Master Fred was
almost the only friend and associate of poor little Mrs. Feathertop, whom he fed daily with meal and water, and only interrupted her sad reflections by pulling her up occasionally
to see how the eggs were coming on.

At last, "Peep, peep, peep!" began to be heard in the nest,
and one little downy head after another poked forth from
under the feathers, surveying the world with round, bright,
winking eyes; and gradually the brood were hatched, and
Mrs. Feathertop arose, a proud and happy mother, with all
the bustling, scratching, care-taking instincts of family-life
warm within her breast. She clucked and scratched, and
cuddled the little downy bits of things as handily and dis-
creetly as a seven-year-old hen could have done, exciting
thereby the wonder of the community.

Master Gray Cock came home in high spirits, and complimented her; told her she was looking charmingly once
more, and said, "Very well, very nice!" as he surveyed the
young brood. So that Mrs Feathertop began to feel the

world going well with her, — when suddenly in came Dame
Scratchard and Goody Kertarkut to make a morning call.

"Let's see the chicks," said Dame Scratchard.

"Goodness me," said Goody Kertarkut, "what a likeness
to their dear papa!"

"Well, but bless me, what's the matter with their bills?"
said Dame Scratchard. "Why, my dear, these chicks are
deformed! I'm sorry for you, my dear, but it's all the result
of your inexperience; you ought to have eaten pebble-stones
with your meal when you were setting. Don't you see,
Dame Kertarkut, what bills they have? That'll increase,
and they'll be frightful!"

"What shall I do?" said Mrs. Feathertop, now greatly
alarmed.

"Nothing, as I know of," said Dame Scratchard, "since
you did n't come to me before you set. I could have told
you all about it. Maybe it won't kill 'em, but they'll always be deformed."

And so the gossips departed, leaving a sting under the
pin-feathers of the poor little hen mamma, who began to
see that her darlings had curious little spoon-bills, different
from her own, and to worry and fret about it.

"My dear," she said to her spouse, "do get Dr. Peppercorn to come in and look at their bills, and see if anything
can be done."

"Dr. Peppercorn came in, and put on a monstrous pair

of spectacles, and said, "Hum! Ha! Extraordinary case,--
very singular!"

"Did you ever see anything like it, Doctor?" said both
parents, in a breath.

"I've read of such cases. It's a calcareous enlargement
of the vascular bony tissue, threatening ossification," said
the Doctor.

"O, dreadful! — can it be possible?" shrieked both parents.
"Can anything be done?"

"Well, I should recommend a daily lotion made of mosquitoes' horns and bicarbonate of frogs' toes, together with a
powder, to be taken morning and night, of muriate of fleas.
One thing you must be careful about: they must never wet
their feet, nor drink any water."

"Dear me, Doctor, I don't know what I *shall* do, for they
seem to have a particular fancy for getting into water."

"Yes, a morbid tendency often found in these cases of
bony tumification of the vascular tissue of the mouth; but
you must resist it, ma'am, as their life depends upon it"; —
and with that Dr. Peppercorn glared gloomily on the young
ducks, who were stealthily poking the objectionable little
spoon-bills out from under their mother's feathers.

After this poor Mrs. Feathertop led a weary life of it; for
the young fry were as healthy and enterprising a brood of
young ducks as ever carried saucepans on the end of their
noses, and they most utterly set themselves against the

Doctor's prescriptions, murmured at the muriate of fleas and the bicarbonate of frogs' toes, and took every opportunity to waddle their little ways down to the mud and water which was in their near vicinity. So their bills grew larger and larger, as did the rest of their bodies, and family government grew weaker and weaker.

"You'll wear me out, children, you certainly will," said poor Mrs. Feathertop.

"You'll go to destruction, — do ye hear?" said Master Gray Cock.

"Did you ever see such frights as poor Mrs. Feathertop has got?" said Dame Scratchard. "I knew what would come of *her* family, — all deformed, and with a dreadful sort of madness, which makes them love to shovel mud with those shocking spoon-bills of theirs."

"It's a kind of idiocy," said Goody Kertarkut. "Poor things! they can't be kept from the water, nor made to take powders, and so they get worse and worse."

"I understand it's affecting their feet so that they can't walk, and a dreadful sort of net is growing between their toes; what a shocking visitation!"

"She brought it on herself," said Dame Scratchard. "Why didn't she come to me before she set? She was always an upstart, self-conceited thing, but I'm sure I pity her."

Meanwhile the young ducks throve apace. Their necks grew glossy, like changeable green and gold satin, and though they would not take the doctor's medicine, and would waddle in the mud and water, — for which they always felt themselves to be very naughty ducks, — yet they grew quite vigorous and hearty. At last one day the whole little tribe waddled off down to the bank of the river. It was a beautiful day, and the river was dancing and dimpling and winking as the little breezes shook the trees that hung over it.

"Well," said the biggest of the little ducks, "in spite of Dr. Peppercorn, I can't help longing for the water. I don't believe it is going to hurt me, — at any rate, here goes"; — and in he plumped, and in went every duck after him, and they threw out their great brown feet as cleverly as if they had taken rowing lessons all their lives, and sailed off on the river, away, away among the ferns, under the pink azalias, through reeds and rushes, and arrow-heads and pickerel-weed, the happiest ducks that ever were born ; and soon they were quite out of sight.

"Well, Mrs. Feathertop, this is a dispensation!" said Mrs. Scratchard. "Your children are all drowned at last, just as I knew they'd be. The old music-teacher, Master Bullfrog, that lives down in Water-Dock Lane, saw 'em all plump madly into the water together this morning ; that's what comes of not knowing how to bring up a family."

Mrs. Feathertop gave only one shriek and fainted dead away, and was carried home on a cabbage-leaf, and Mr.

Gray Cock was sent for, where he was waiting on Mrs. Red Comb through the squash-vines.

"It's a serious time in your family, sir," said Goody Kertarkut, "and you ought to be at home supporting your wife. Send for Doctor Peppercorn without delay."

Now as the case was a very dreadful one, Doctor Peppercorn called a council from the barn-yard of the Squire, two miles off, and a brisk young Doctor Partlett appeared, in a fine suit of brown and gold, with tail-feathers like meteors. A fine young fellow he was, lately from Paris, with all the modern scientific improvements fresh in his head.

When he had listened to the whole story, he clapped his spur into the ground, and leaning back, laughed so loud that all the cocks in the neighborhood crowed.

Mrs. Feathertop rose up out of her swoon, and Mr. Gray Cock was greatly enraged.

"What do you mean, sir, by such behavior in the house of mourning?"

"My dear sir, pardon me, — but there is no occasion for mourning. My dear madam, let me congratulate you. There is no harm done. The simple matter is, dear madam, you have been under a hallucination all along. The neighborhood and my learned friend the doctor have all made a mistake in thinking that these children of yours were hens at all. They are ducks, ma'am, evidently ducks, and very finely formed ducks I dare say."

At this moment a quack was heard, and at a distance the whole tribe were seen coming waddling home, their feathers gleaming in green and gold, and they themselves in high good spirits.

"Such a splendid day as we have had!" they all cried in a breath. "And we know now how to get our own living; we can take care of ourselves in future, so you need have no further trouble with us."

"Madam," said the doctor, making a bow with an air which displayed his tail-feathers to advantage, "let me congratulate you on the charming family you have raised. A finer brood of young, healthy ducks I never saw. Give claw, my dear friend," he said, addressing the elder son. "In our barn-yard no family is more respected than that of the ducks."

And so Madam Feathertop came off glorious at last; and when after this the ducks used to go swimming up and down the river like so many nabobs among the admiring hens, Doctor Peppercorn used to look after them and say, "Ah! I had the care of their infancy!" and Mr. Gray Cock and his wife used to say, "It was our system of education did that!"

THE NUTCRACKERS OF NUTCRACKER LODGE.

MR. and Mrs. Nutcracker were as respectable a pair of squirrels as ever wore gray brushes over their backs. They were animals of a settled and serious turn of mind, not disposed to run after vanities and novelties, but filling their station in life with prudence and sobriety. Nutcracker Lodge was a hole in a sturdy old chestnut overhanging a shady dell, and was held to be as respectably kept an establishment as there was in the whole forest. Even Miss Jenny Wren, the greatest gossip of the neighborhood, never found anything to criticise in its arrange-

ments, and old Parson Too-whit, a venerable owl who inhabited a branch somewhat more exalted, as became his pro-
fession, was in the habit of saving himself much trouble in
his parochial exhortations by telling his parishioners in short
to "look at the Nutcrackers" if they wanted to see what it
was to live a virtuous life.　Everything had gone on prosperously with them, and they had reared many successive
families of young Nutcrackers, who went forth to assume
their places in the forest of life, and to reflect credit on
their bringing-up, — so that naturally enough they began
to have a very easy way of considering themselves models
of wisdom.

But at last it came along, in the course of events, that
they had a son named Featherhead, who was destined to
bring them a great deal of anxiety.　Nobody knows what
the reason is, but the fact was, that Master Featherhead
was as different from all the former children of this worthy
couple as if he had been dropped out of the moon into
their nest, instead of coming into it in the general way.
Young Featherhead was a squirrel of good parts and a
lively disposition, but he was sulky and contrary and unreasonable, and always finding matter of complaint in everything his respectable papa and mamma did.　Instead of
assisting in the cares of a family, — picking up nuts and
learning other lessons proper to a young squirrel, — he
seemed to settle himself from his earliest years into a sort

of lofty contempt for the Nutcrackers, for Nutcracker
Lodge, and for all the good old ways and institutions of
the domestic hole, which he declared to be stupid and
unreasonable, and entirely behind the times.   To be sure,
he was always on hand at meal-times, and played a very
lively tooth on the nuts which his mother had collected,
always selecting the very best for himself; but he seasoned
his nibbling with so much grumbling and discontent, and
so many severe remarks, as to give the impression that he
considered himself a peculiarly ill-used squirrel in having
to "eat their old grub," as he very unceremoniously
called it.

Papa Nutcracker, on these occasions, was often fiercely
indignant, and poor little Mamma Nutcracker would shed
tears, and beg her darling to be a little more reasonable ;
but the young gentleman seemed always to consider himself as the injured party.

Now nobody could tell why or wherefore Master Featherhead looked upon himself as injured and aggrieved, since
he was living in a good hole, with plenty to eat, and without the least care or labor of his own ; but he seemed
rather to value himself upon being gloomy and dissatis-
fied.   While his parents and brothers and sisters were
cheerfully racing up and down the branches, busy in their
domestic toils, and laying up stores for the winter, Featherhead sat gloomily apart, declaring himself weary of exist-

ence, and feeling himself at liberty to quarrel with everybody and everything about him. Nobody understood him,
he said ; — he was a squirrel of a peculiar nature, and
needed peculiar treatment, and nobody treated him in a
way that did not grate on the finer nerves of his feelings.
He had higher notions of existence than could be bounded
by that old rotten hole in a hollow tree ; he had thoughts
that soared far above the miserable, petty details of every-
day life, and he *could* not and *would* not bring down these
soaring aspirations to the contemptible toil of laying up a
few chestnuts or hickory-nuts for winter.

"Depend upon it, my dear," said Mrs. Nutcracker solemnly, "that fellow must be a genius."

"Fiddlestick on his genius!" said old Mr. Nutcracker ;
"what does he *do ?*"

"O nothing, of course ; that's one of the first marks of
genius. Geniuses, you know, never can come down to
common life."

"He eats enough for any two," remarked old Nutcracker,
"and he never helps gather nuts."

"My dear, ask Parson Too-whit ; he has conversed with
him, and quite agrees with me that he says very uncommon things for a squirrel of his age ; he has such fine
feelings, — so much above those of the common crowd."

"Fine feelings be hanged!" said old Nutcracker. "When
a fellow eats all the nuts that his mother gives him, and

then grumbles at her, I don't believe much in his fine feelings. Why don't he set himself about something? I'm
going to tell my fine young gentleman, that, if he does n't
behave himself, I'll tumble him out of the nest, neck and
crop, and see if hunger won't do something towards bringing down his fine airs."

But then Mrs. Nutcracker fell on her husband's neck
with both paws, and wept, and besought him so piteously
to have patience with her darling, that old Nutcracker,
who was himself a soft-hearted old squirrel, was prevailed
upon to put up with the airs and graces of his young scape-
grace a little longer; and secretly in his silly old heart
he revolved the question whether possibly it might not
be that a great genius was actually to come of his household.

The Nutcrackers belonged to the old established race of
the Grays, but they were sociable, friendly people, and kept
on the best of terms with all branches of the Nutcracker
family. The Chipmunks of Chipmunk Hollow were a very
lively, cheerful, sociable race, and on the very best of terms
with the Nutcracker Grays. Young Tip Chipmunk, the
oldest son, was in all respects a perfect contrast to Master
Featherhead. He was always lively and cheerful, and so
very alert in providing for the family, that old Mr. and
Mrs. Chipmunk had very little care, but could sit sociably
at the door of their hole and chat with neighbors, quite

sure that Tip would bring everything out right for them, and have plenty laid up for winter.

Now Featherhead took it upon him, for some reason or other, to look down upon Tip Chipmunk, and on every occasion to disparage him in the social circle, as a very common kind of squirrel, with whom it would be best not to associate too freely.

"My dear," said Mrs. Nutcracker one day, when he was. expressing these ideas, "it seems to me that you are too hard on poor Tip; he is a most excellent son and brother, and I wish you would be civil to him."

"O, I don't doubt that Tip is *good* enough," said Featherhead, carelessly; "but then he is so very common! he hasn't an idea in his skull above his nuts and his hole. He is good-natured enough, to be sure, — these very ordinary people often are good-natured, — but he wants manner; he has really no manner at all; and as to the deeper feelings, Tip hasn't the remotest idea of them. I mean always to be civil to Tip when he comes in my way, but I think the less we see of that sort of people the better; and I hope, mother, you won't invite the Chipmunks at Christmas, — these family dinners are such a bore!"

"But, my dear, your father thinks a great deal of the Chipmunks; and it is an old family custom to have all the relatives here at Christmas."

"And an awful bore it is! Why must people of refinement and elevation be forever tied down because of some distant relationship?   Now there are our cousins the High-Flyers, — if we could get them, there would be some sense in it.   Young Whisk rather promised me for Christmas; but it's seldom now you can get a flying squirrel to show himself in our parts, and if we are intimate with the Chip-munks it is n't to be expected."

"Confound him for a puppy!" said old Nutcracker, when his wife repeated these sayings to him.   "Featherhead is a fool.   Common, forsooth!   I wish good, industrious, pains-taking sons like Tip Chipmunk *were* common.   For my part, I find these uncommon people the most. tiresome; they are not content with letting us carry the whole load, but they sit on it, and scold at us while we carry them."

But old Mr. Nutcracker, like many other good old gen-tlemen squirrels, found that Christmas dinners and other things were apt to go as his wife said, and his wife was apt to go as young Featherhead said; and so, when Christ-mas came, the Chipmunks were not invited, for the first time in many years.   The Chipmunks, however, took all pleasantly, and accepted poor old Mrs. Nutcracker's awk-ward apologies with the best possible grace, and young Tip looked in on Christmas morning with the compliments of the season and a few beech-nuts, which he had secured as a great dainty.   The fact was, that Tip's little striped fur coat was so filled up and overflowing with cheerful

good-will to all, that he never could be made to understand that any of his relations could want to cut him;
and therefore Featherhead looked down on him with contempt, and said he had no tact, and could n't see when
he was not wanted.

It was wonderful to see how, by means of persisting in
remarks like these, young Featherhead at last got all his
family to look up to him as something uncommon. Though
he added nothing to the family, and required more to be
done for him than all the others put together, — though he
showed not the smallest real perseverance or ability in anything useful, — yet somehow all his brothers and sisters,
and his poor foolish old mother, got into a way of regard-
ing him as something wonderful, and delighting in his
sharp sayings as if they had been the wisest things in the
world.

But at last old papa declared that it was time for Featherhead to settle himself to some business in life, roundly
declaring that he could not always have him as a hanger-
on in the paternal hole.

"What are you going to do, my boy?" said Tip Chipmunk to him one day. "We are driving now a thriving
trade in hickory-nuts, and if you would like to join us — "

"Thank you," said Featherhead; "but I confess I have
no fancy for anything so slow as the hickory trade; I
never was made to grub and delve in that way."

The fact was, that Featherhead had lately been forming alliances such as no reputable squirrel should even think of. He had more than once been seen going out evenings with the Rats of Rat Hollow, — a race whose reputation for honesty was more than doubtful. The fact was, further, that old Longtooth Rat, an old sharper and money-lender, had long had his eye on Featherhead as just about silly enough for their purposes, — engaging him in what he called a speculation, but which was neither more nor less than downright stealing.

Near by the chestnut-tree where Nutcracker Lodge was situated was a large barn filled with corn and grain, besides many bushels of hazel-nuts, chestnuts, and walnuts. Now old Longtooth proposed to young Featherhead that he should nibble a passage into this loft, and there establish himself in the commission business, passing the nuts and corn to him as he wanted them. Old Longtooth knew what he was about in the proposal, for he had heard talk of a brisk Scotch terrier that was about to be bought to keep the rats from the grain ; but you may be sure he kept his knowledge to himself, so that Featherhead was none the wiser for it.

"The nonsense of fellows like Tip Chipmunk!" said Featherhead to his admiring brothers and sisters. "The perfectly stupid nonsense! There he goes, delving and poking, picking up a nut here and a grain there, when _I_ step into property at once."

"But I hope, my son, you are careful to be honest in your dealings," said old Nutcracker, who was a very moral squirrel.

With that, young Featherhead threw his tail saucily over one shoulder, winked knowingly at his brothers, and said, "Certainly, sir! If honesty consists in getting what you can while it is going, I mean to be honest."

Very soon Featherhead appeared to his admiring companions in the height of prosperity. He had a splendid hole in the midst of a heap of chestnuts, and he literally seemed to be rolling in wealth; he never came home without showering lavish gifts on his mother and sisters; he wore his tail over his back with a buckish air, and patronized Tip Chipmunk with a gracious nod whenever he met him, and thought that the world was going well with him.

But one luckless day, as Featherhead was lolling in his hole, up came two boys with the friskiest, wiriest Scotch terrier you ever saw. His eyes blazed like torches, and poor Featherhead's heart died within him as he heard the boys say, "Now we'll see if we can't catch the rascal that eats our grain."

Featherhead tried to slink out at the hole he had gnawed to come in by, but found it stopped.

"O, you are there, are you, Mister?" said the boy. "Well, you don't get out; and now for a chase!"

And, sure enough, poor Featherhead ran distracted with

terror up and down, through the bundles of hay, between barrels, and over casks; but with the barking terrier ever at his heels, and the boys running, shouting, and cheering his pursuer on. He was glad at last to escape through a crack, though he left half of his fine brush behind him, — for Master Wasp the terrier made a snap at it just as he was going, and cleaned all the hair off of it, so that it was bare as a rat's tail.

Poor Featherhead limped off, bruised and beaten and be-draggled, with the boys and dog still after him; and they would have caught him, after all, if Tip Chipmunk's hole had not stood hospitably open to receive him. Tip took him in, like a good-natured fellow as he was, and took the best of care of him ; but the glory of Featherhead's tail had departed forever. He had sprained his left paw, and got a chronic rheumatism, and the fright and fatigue which he had gone through had broken up his constitution, so that he never again could be what he had been ; but Tip gave him a situation as under-clerk in his establishment, and from that time he was a sadder and a wiser squirrel than he ever had been before.

THE HISTORY OF TIP-TOP.

UNDER the window of a certain pretty little cottage there grew a great old apple-tree, which in the spring had thousands and thousands of lovely pink blossoms on it, and in the autumn had about half as many bright red apples as it had blossoms in the spring.

The nursery of this cottage was a little bower of a room, papered with mossy-green paper, and curtained with white muslin ; and here five little children used to come, in their white nightgowns, to be dressed and have their hair brushed and curled every morning

First, there were Alice and Mary, bright-eyed, laughing little girls, of seven and eight years, and then came stout little Jamie, and Charlie, and finally little Puss, whose real name was Ellen, but who was called Puss, and Pussy, and Birdie, and Toddlie, and any other pet name that came to mind.

Now it used to happen, every morning, that the five little heads would be peeping out of the window, together, into the flowery boughs of the apple-tree ; and the reason was this. A pair of robins had built a very pretty, smooth-lined nest in a fork of the limb that came directly under the window, and the building of this nest had been superintended, day by day, by the five pairs of bright eyes of these five children. The robins at first had been rather shy of this inspection ; but, as they got better acquainted, they seemed to think no more of the little curly heads in the window, than of the pink blossoms about them, or the daisies and buttercups at the foot of the tree.

All the little hands were forward to help ; some threw out flossy bits of cotton, — for which, we grieve to say, Charlie had cut a hole in the crib quilt, — and some threw out bits of thread and yarn, and Allie ravelled out a considerable piece from one of her garters, which she threw out as a contribution ; and they exulted in seeing the skill with which the little builders wove everything in. "Little birds, little birds," they would say, "you shall be kept warm, for we have given you cotton out of our crib quilt, and yarn

out of our stockings." Nay, so far did this generosity pro-
ceed, that Charlie cut a flossy, golden curl from Toddlie's
head and threw it out ; and when the birds caught it up
the whole flock laughed to see Toddlie's golden hair figur-
ing in a bird's-nest.

When the little thing was finished, it was so neat, and
trim, and workman-like, that the children all exulted over
it, and called it "our nest," and the two robins they called
"our birds." But wonderful was the joy when the little
eyes, opening one morning, saw in the nest a beautiful pale-
green egg ; and the joy grew from day to day, for every
day there came another egg, and so on till there were five
little eggs ; and then the oldest girl, Alice, said, "There
are five eggs ; that makes one for each of us, and each of
us will have a little bird by and by" ; — at which all the
children laughed and jumped for glee.

When the five little eggs were all laid, the mother-bird
began to sit on them ; and at any time of day or night,
when a little head peeped out of the nursery window, might
be seen a round, bright, patient pair of bird's eyes contentedly waiting for the young birds to come. It seemed a long
time for the children to wait ; but every day they put some
bread and cake from their luncheon on the window-sill, so
that the birds might have something to eat ; but still there
she was, patiently watching !

"How long, long, long she waits !" said Jamie, impatiently.
"I don't believe she's ever going to hatch."

"O, yes she is!" said grave little Alice. "Jamie, you don't understand about these things ; it takes a long, long time to hatch eggs. Old Sam says his hens set three weeks ; — only think, almost a month!"

Three weeks looked a long time to the five bright pairs of little watching eyes ; but Jamie said, the eggs were so much smaller than hens' eggs, that it would n't take so long to hatch them, he knew. Jamie always thought he knew all about everything, and was so sure of it that he rather took the lead among the children. But one morning, when they pushed their five heads out of the window, the round, patient little bird-eyes were gone, and there seemed to be nothing in the nest but a bunch of something hairy.

Upon this they all cried out, "O mamma, *do* come here! the bird is gone and left her nest!" And when they cried out, they saw five wide little red mouths open in the nest, and saw that the hairy bunch of stuff was indeed the first of five little birds.

"They are dreadful-looking things," said Mary ; "I did n't know that little birds began by looking so badly."

"They seem to be all mouth," said Jamie.

"We must feed them," said Charlie.

"Here, little birds, here's some gingerbread for you," he said ; and he threw a bit of his gingerbread, which fortunately only hit the nest on the outside, and fell down among the buttercups, where two crickets made a meal of it, and

agreed that it was as excellent gingerbread as if old Mother
Cricket herself had made it.

"Take care, Charlie," said his mamma; "we do not know
enough to feed young birds. We must leave it to their
papa and mamma, who probably started out bright and
early in the morning to get breakfast for them."

Sure enough, while they were speaking, back came Mr.
and Mrs. Robin, whirring through the green shadows of
the apple-tree; and thereupon all the five little red mouths
flew open, and the birds put something into each.

It was great amusement, after this, to watch the daily
feeding of the little birds, and to observe how, when not
feeding them, the mother sat brooding on the nest, warm-
ing them under her soft wings, while the father-bird sat on
the tip-top bough of the apple-tree and sang to them. In
time they grew and grew, and, instead of a nest full of
little red mouths, there was a nest full of little, fat, speckled
robins, with round, bright, cunning eyes, just like their
parents; and the children began to talk together about
their birds.

"I 'm going to give my robin a name," said Mary. "I
call him Brown-Eyes."

"And I call mine Tip-Top," said Jamie, "because I
know he 'll be a tip-top bird."

"And I call mine singer," said Alice.

"I 'all mine Toddy," said little Toddlie, who would not
be behindhand in anything that was going on.

"Hurrah for Toddlie!" said Charlie, "her's is the best of all. For my part, I call mine Speckle."

So then the birds were all made separate characters by having each a separate name given it. Brown-Eyes, Tip-Top, Singer, Toddy, and Speckle made, as they grew bigger, a very crowded nestful of birds.

Now the children had early been taught to say in a little hymn : —

> "Birds in their little nests agree,
> And 't is a shameful sight
> When children of one family
> Fall out, and chide, and fight"; —

and they thought anything really written and printed in a hymn must be true ; therefore they were very much astonished to see, from day to day, that *their* little birds in their nests did *not* agree.

Tip-Top was the biggest and strongest bird, and he was always shuffling and crowding the others, and clamoring for the most food ; and when Mrs. Robin came in with a nice bit of anything, Tip-Top's red mouth opened so wide, and he was so noisy, that one would think the nest was all his. His mother used to correct him for these gluttonous ways, and sometimes made him wait till all the rest were helped before she gave him a mouthful ; but he generally revenged himself in her absence by crowding the others and making the nest generally uncomfortable. Speckle, however, was a bird of spirit, and he used to peck at Tip-Top; so they would sometimes have a regular sparring-match across poor Brown-Eyes, who was a meek, tender little fellow, and would sit winking and blinking in fear while his big brothers quarrelled. As to Toddy and Sing-er, they turned out to be sister birds, and showed quite a feminine talent for chattering; they used to scold their badly behaving brothers in a way that made the nest quite lively.

On the whole, Mr. and Mrs. Robin did not find their family circle the peaceable place the poet represents.

"I say," said Tip-Top one day to them, "this old nest is a dull, mean, crowded hole, and it's quite time some of us were out of it; just give us lessons in flying, won't you, and let us go."

"My dear boy," said Mother Robin, "we shall teach you to fly as soon as your wings are strong enough."

"You are a very little bird," said his father, "and ought to be good and obedient, and wait patiently till your wing-feathers grow; and then you can soar away to some purpose."

"Wait for my wing-feathers? Humbug!" Tip-Top would say, as he sat balancing with his little short tail on the edge of the nest, and looking down through the grass and clover-heads below, and up into the blue clouds above. "Father and mother are slow old birds; keep a fellow

back with their confounded notions.   If they don't hurry
up, I 'll take matters into my own claws, and be off some
day before they know it.   Look at those swallows, skim-
ming and diving through the blue air!   That 's the way
I want to do."

"But, dear brother, the way to learn to do that is to be
good and obedient while we are little, and wait till our
parents think it best for us to begin."

"Shut up your preaching," said Tip-Top; "what do you
girls know of flying?"

"About as much as *you*," said Speckle.   "However, I 'm
sure I don't care how soon you take yourself off, for you
take up more room than all the rest put together."

"You mind yourself, Master Speckle, or you 'll get something you don't like," said Tip-Top, still strutting in a very
cavalier way on the edge of the nest, and sticking up his
little short tail quite valiantly.

"O my darlings," said the mamma, now fluttering home,
"cannot I ever teach you to live in love?"

"It 's all Tip-Top's fault," screamed the other birds in a
flutter.

"My fault? Of course, everything in this nest that goes
wrong is laid to me," said Tip-Top; "and I 'll leave it to
anybody, now, if I crowd anybody.   I 've been sitting outside, on the very edge of the nest, and there 's Speckle
has got my place."

3

"Who wants your place?" said Speckle. "I 'm sure
you can come in, if you please."

"My dear boy," said the mother, "do go into the nest
and be a good little bird, and then you will be happy."

"That 's always the talk," said Tip-Top. "I 'm too big
for the nest, and I want to see the world. It 's full of
beautiful things, I know. Now there 's the most lovely
creature, with bright eyes, that comes under the tree every
day, and wants me to come down in the grass and play
with her."

"My son, my son, beware!" said the frightened mother;
"that lovely seeming creature is our dreadful enemy, the
cat,— a horrid monster, with teeth and claws."

At this, all the little birds shuddered and cuddled deeper
in the nest; only Tip-Top, in his heart, disbelieved it.
"I 'm too old a bird," said he to himself, "to believe *that*
story; mother is chaffing me. But I 'll show her that I
can take care of myself."

So the next morning, after the father and mother were
gone, Tip-Top got on the edge of the nest again, and
looked over and saw lovely Miss Pussy washing her face
among the daisies under the tree, and her hair was sleek
and white as the daisies, and her eyes were yellow and
beautiful to behold, and she looked up to the tree be-
witchingly, and said, "Little birds, little birds, come down;
Pussy wants to play with you."

"Only look at her!" said Tip-Top; "her eyes are like gold."

"No, don't look," said Singer and Speckle. "She will bewitch you and then eat you up."

"I'd like to see her try to eat me up," said Tip-Top, again balancing his short tail over the nest. "Just as if she would. She's just the nicest, most innocent creature going, and only wants us to have fun. We never do have any fun in this old nest!"

Then the yellow eyes below shot a bewildering light into Tip-Top's eyes, and a voice sounded sweet as silver: "Little birds, little birds, come down; Pussy wants to play with you."

"Her paws are as white as velvet," said Tip-Top; "and so soft! I don't believe she has any claws."

"Don't go, brother, don't!" screamed both sisters.

All we know about it is, that a moment after a direful scream was heard from the nursery window. "O mamma, mamma, do come here! Tip-Top's fallen out of the nest, and the cat has got him!"

Away ran Pussy with foolish little Tip-Top in her mouth, and he squeaked dolefully when he felt her sharp teeth. Wicked Miss Pussy had no mind to eat him at once; she meant just as she said, to "play with him." So she ran off to a private place among the currant-bushes, while all the little curly heads were scattered up and down looking for her

Did you ever see a cat play with a bird or a mouse? She sets it down, and seems to go off and leave it; but the moment it makes the first movement to get away, — pounce! she springs on it, and shakes it in her mouth; and so she teases and tantalizes it, till she gets ready to kill and eat it. I can't say why she does it, except that it is a cat's nature; and it is a very bad nature for foolish young robins to get acquainted with.

"O, where is he? where is he? Do find my poor Tip-Top," said Jamie, crying as loud as he could scream. "I'll kill that horrid cat, — I'll kill her!"

Mr. and Mrs. Robin, who had come home meantime, joined their plaintive chirping to the general confusion; and Mrs. Robin's bright eyes soon discovered her poor little son, where Pussy was patting and rolling him from one paw to the other under the currant-bushes; and settling on the bush above, she called the little folks to the spot by her cries.

Jamie plunged under the bush, and caught the cat with luckless Tip-Top in her mouth; and, with one or two good thumps, he obliged her to let him go. Tip-Top was not dead, but in a sadly draggled and torn state. Some of his feathers were torn out, and one of his wings was broken, and hung down in a melancholy way.

"O, what *shall* we do for him? He will die. Poor Tip-Top!" said the children.

"Let's put him back into the nest, children," said mamma. "His mother will know best what to do with him."

So a ladder was got, and papa climbed up and put poor Tip-Top safely into the nest. The cat had shaken all the nonsense well out of him ; he was a dreadfully humbled young robin.

The time came at last when all the other birds in the nest learned to fly, and fluttered and flew about everywhere ; but poor melancholy Tip-Top was still confined to the nest with a broken wing. Finally, as it became evident that it would be long before he could fly, Jamie took him out of the nest, and made a nice little cage for him, and used to feed him every day, and he would hop about and seem tolerably contented ; but it was evident that he would be a lame-winged robin all his days.

Jamie's mother told him that Tip-Top's history was an allegory.

"I don't know what you mean, mamma," said Jamie.

"When something in a bird's life is like something in a boy's life, or when a story is similar in its meaning to reality, we call it an allegory. Little boys, when they are about half grown up, sometimes do just as Tip-Top did. They are in a great hurry to get away from home into the great world ; and then Temptation comes, with bright eyes and smooth velvet paws, and promises them fun; and they go to bad places; they get to smoking, and then to drinking; and, finally, the bad habit gets them in its teeth and claws, and plays with them as a cat does with a mouse. They try to reform, just as your robin tried to get away from the cat; but their bad habits pounce on them and drag them back. And so, when the time comes that they want to begin life, they are miserable, broken-down creatures, like your broken-winged robin.

" So, Jamie, remember, and don't try to be a man before your time, and let your parents judge for you while you are young; and never believe in any soft white Pussy, with golden eyes, that comes and wants to tempt you to come down and play with her. If a big boy offers to teach you to smoke a cigar, that is Pussy. If a boy wants you to go into a billiard-saloon, that is Pussy. If a boy wants you to learn to drink anything with spirit in it, however sweetened and disguised, remember, Pussy is there; and Pussy's claws are long, and Pussy's teeth are strong; and if she gives you one shake in your youth, you will be like a broken-winged robin all your days."

MISS KATY–DID AND MISS CRICKET.

MISS KATY–DID sat on the branch of a flowering Azalia, in her best suit of fine green and silver, with wings of point-lace from Mother Nature's finest web.

Miss Katy was in the very highest possible spirits, because her gallant cousin, Colonel Katy-did, had looked in to make her a morning visit. It was a fine morning, too, which goes for as much among the Katy-dids as among men and women. It was, in fact, a morning that Miss Katy thought must have been made on purpose for her to enjoy herself in. There had been a patter of rain the night before, which had kept the leaves awake talking to each other till nearly morning, but by dawn the small winds had blown brisk little puffs, and whisked the heavens clear and bright with their tiny wings, as you have seen Susan clear away the cobwebs in your mamma's parlor; and so now there were only left a thousand blinking, burning water-drops, hanging like convex mirrors at the end of each leaf, and Miss Katy admired herself in each one.

"Certainly I am a pretty creature," she said to herself; and when the gallant Colonel said something about being dazzled by her beauty, she only tossed her head and took it as quite a matter of course.

"The fact is, my dear Colonel," she said, "I am thinking of giving a party, and you must help me make out the lists."

"My dear, you make me the happiest of Katy-dids."

"Now," said Miss Katy-did, drawing an azalia-leaf towards her, "let us see,—whom shall we have? The Fireflies, of course; everybody wants them, they are so brilliant;—a little unsteady, to be sure, but quite in the higher circles."

"Yes, we must have the Fireflies," echoed the Colonel.

"Well, then,—and the Butterflies and the Moths. Now, there 's a trouble. There 's such an everlasting tribe of those Moths; and if you invite dull people they 're always sure all to come, every one of them. Still, if you have the Butterflies, you can't leave out the Moths.

"Old Mrs. Moth has been laid up lately with a gastric fever, and that may keep two or three of the Misses Moth at home," said the Colonel.

"Whatever could give the old lady such a turn?" said Miss Katy. "I thought she never was sick."

"I suspect it 's high living. I understand she and her family ate up a whole ermine cape last month, and it disagreed with them.

"For my part, I can't conceive how the Moths can live as they do," said Miss Katy, with a face of disgust. Why, I could no more eat worsted and fur, as they do—"

"That is quite evident from the fairy-like delicacy of

your appearance," said the Colonel. "One can see that nothing so gross or material has ever entered into your system."

"I 'm sure," said Miss Katy, "mamma says she don't
know what does keep me alive; half a dewdrop and a
little bit of the nicest part of a rose-leaf, I assure you,
often last me for a day. But we are forgetting our list.
Let 's see, — the Fireflies, Butterflies, Moths. The Bees
must come, I suppose."

"The Bees are a worthy family," said the Colonel.

"Worthy enough, but dreadfully humdrum," said Miss
Katy. They never talk about anything but honey and
housekeeping; still, they are a class of people one cannot
neglect."

"Well, then, there are the Bumble-Bees."

"O, I doat on them! General Bumble is one of the
most dashing, brilliant fellows of the day."

"I think he is shockingly corpulent," said Colonel Katy-
did, not at all pleased to hear him praised;—"don't you?"

"I don't know but he *is* a little stout," said Miss Katy;
"but so distinguished and elegant in his manners, — something martial and breezy about him."

"Well, if you invite the Bumble-Bees you must have
the Hornets."

"Those spiteful Hornets, — I detest them!"

"Nevertheless, dear Miss Katy, one does not like to
offend the Hornets."

"No, one can't. There are those five Misses Hornet, —
dreadful old maids! — as full of spite as they can live.
You may be sure they will every one come, and be looking about to make spiteful remarks. Put down the Hornets, though."

"How about the Mosquitos!" said the Colonel.

"Those horrid Mosquitos, — they are dreadfully plebeian!
Can't one cut them?"

"Well, dear Miss Katy," said the Colonel, "if you ask
my candid opinion as a friend, I should say *not*. There's
young Mosquito, who graduated last year, has gone into
literature, and is connected with some of our leading pa-
pers, and they say he carries the sharpest pen of all the
writers. It won't do to offend him."

"And so I suppose we must have his old aunts, and all
six of his sisters, and all his dreadfully common relations."

"It is a pity," said the Colonel, "but one must pay
one's tax to society."

Just at this moment the conference was interrupted by
a visitor, Miss Keziah Cricket, who came in with her work-
bag on her arm to ask a subscription for a poor family of
Ants who had just had their house hoed up in clearing the
garden-walks.

"How stupid of them," said Katy, "not to know better
than to put their house in the garden-walk; that 's just
like those Ants!"

"Well, they are in great trouble; all their stores destroyed, and their father killed, — cut quite in two by a hoe."

"How very shocking! I don't like to hear of such disagreeable things, — it affects my nerves terribly. Well, I'm sure I have n't anything to give. Mamma said yesterday she was sure she did n't know how our bills were to be paid, — and there's my green satin with point-lace yet to come home." And Miss Katy-did shrugged her shoulders and affected to be very busy with Colonel Katy-did, in just the way that young ladies sometimes do when they wish to signify to visitors that they had better leave.

Little Miss Cricket perceived how the case stood, and so hopped briskly off, without giving herself even time to be offended. "Poor extravagant little thing!" said she to herself, "it was hardly worth while to ask her."

"Pray, shall you invite the Crickets?" said Colonel Katy-did.

"Who? I? Why, Colonel, what a question! Invite the Crickets? Of what can you be thinking?"

"And shall you not ask the Locusts, or the Grasshoppers?"

"Certainly. The Locusts, of course, — a very old and distinguished family; and the Grasshoppers are pretty well, and ought to be asked. But we must draw a line somewhere, — and the Crickets! why, it's shocking even to think of!"

"I thought they were nice, respectable people."

"O, perfectly nice and respectable, — very good people, in fact, so far as that goes. But then you must see the difficulty."

"My dear cousin, I am afraid you must explain."

"Why, their *color*, to be sure. Don't you see?"

"Oh!" said the Colonel. "That's it, is it? Excuse me, but I have been living in France, where these distinctions are wholly unknown, and I have not yet got myself in the train of fashionable ideas here."

"Well, then, let me teach you," said Miss Katy. "You know we republicans go for no distinctions except those created by Nature herself, and we found our rank upon *color*, because that is clearly a thing that none has any hand in but our Maker. You see?"

"Yes; but who decides what color shall be the reigning color?"

"I'm surprised to hear the question! The only true color — the only proper one — is *our* color, to be sure. A lovely pea-green is the precise shade on which to found aristocratic distinction. But then we are liberal; — we associate with the Moths, who are gray; with the Butterflies, who are blue-and-gold-colored; with the Grasshoppers, yellow and brown; — and society would become dreadfully mixed if it were not fortunately ordered that the Crickets are black as jet. The fact is, that a class to be looked

down upon is necessary to all elegant society, and if the
Crickets were not black, we could not keep them down,

because, as everybody knows, they are often a great deal
cleverer than we are. They have a vast talent for music
and dancing; they are very quick at learning, and would
be getting to the very top of the ladder if we once allowed them to climb. But their being black is a conven-
ience, — because, as long as we are green and they black,
we have a superiority that can never be taken from us.
Don't you see, now?"

"O yes, I see exactly," said the Colonel.

"Now that Keziah Cricket, who just came in here, is
quite a musician, and her old father plays the violin beautifully; — by the way, we might engage him for our orchestra."

And so Miss Katy's ball came off, and the performers
kept it up from sundown till daybreak, so that it seemed
as if every leaf in the forest were alive. The Katy-dids,
and the Mosquitos, and the Locusts, and a full orchestra
of Crickets made the air perfectly vibrate, insomuch that
old Parson Too-Whit, who was preaching a Thursday evening lecture to a very small audience, announced to his
hearers that he should certainly write a discourse against
dancing for the next weekly occasion.

The good Doctor was even with his word in the matter, and gave out some very sonorous discourses, without
in the least stopping the round of gayeties kept up by

these dissipated Katy-dids, which ran on, night after night, till the celebrated Jack Frost epidemic, which occurred somewhere about the first of September.

Poor Miss Katy, with her flimsy green satin and point-lace, was one of the first victims, and fell from the bough in company with a sad shower of last year's leaves. The worthy Cricket family, however, avoided Jack Frost by emigrating in time to the chimney-corner of a nice little cottage that had been built in the wood that summer.

There good old Mr. and Mrs. Cricket, with sprightly Miss Keziah and her brothers and sisters, found a warm and welcome home; and when the storm howled without, and lashed the poor naked trees, the Crickets on the warm hearth would chirp out cheery welcome to papa as he came in from the snowy path, or mamma as she sat at her work-basket.

"Cheep, cheep, cheep!" little Freddy would say. "Mamma, who is it says 'cheep'?"

"Dear Freddy, it's our own dear little cricket, who loves us and comes to sing to us when the snow is on the ground."

So when poor Miss Katy-did's satin and lace were all swept away, the warm home-talents of the Crickets made for them a welcome refuge.

MOTHER MAGPIE'S MISCHIEF.

OLD MOTHER MAGPIE was about the busiest character in the forest. But you must know that there
is a great difference between being busy and being industrious. One may be very busy all the time, and yet not
in the least industrious; and this was the case with Mother
Magpie.

She was always full of everybody's business but her own,
— up and down, here and there, everywhere but in her
own nest, knowing every one's affairs, telling what everybody had been doing or ought to do, and ready to cast
her advice *gratis* at every bird and beast of the woods.

Now she bustled up to the parsonage at the top of
the oak-tree, to tell old Parson Too-Whit what she thought
he ought to preach for his next sermon, and how dreadful
the morals of the parish were becoming. Then, having
perfectly bewildered the poor old gentleman, who was always sleepy of a Monday morning, Mother Magpie would
take a peep into Mrs. Oriole's nest, sit chattering on a
bough above, and pour forth floods of advice, which, poor
little Mrs. Oriole used to say to her husband, bewildered
her more than a hard northeast storm.

"Depend upon it, my dear," Mother Magpie would say,

"that this way of building your nest, swinging like an old empty stocking from a bough, is n't at all the thing. I never built one so in my life, and I never have headaches. Now you complain always that your head aches whenever I call upon you. It 's all on account of this way of swinging and swaying about in such an absurd manner."

"But, my dear," piped Mrs. Oriole, timidly, "the Orioles always have built in this manner, and it suits our constitution."

"A fiddle on your constitution! How can you tell what agrees with your constitution unless you try? You own you are not well; you are subject to headaches, and every physician will tell you that a tilting motion disorders the stomach and acts upon the brain. Ask old Dr. Kite. I was talking with him about your case only yesterday, and says he, 'Mrs. Magpie, I perfectly agree with you.'"

"But my husband prefers this style of building."

"That 's only because he is n't properly instructed. Pray, did you ever attend Dr. Kite's lectures on the nervous system?"

"No, I have no time to attend lectures. Who would set on the eggs?"

"Why, your husband, to be sure; don't he take his turn in setting? If he don't, he ought to. I shall speak to him about it. My husband always sets regularly half the time, that I might have time to go about and exercise."

4

"O Mrs. Magpie, pray don't speak to my husband; he will think I 've been complaining."

"No, no, he won't! Let me alone. I understand just how to say the thing. I 've advised hundreds of young husbands in my day, and I never give offence."

"But I tell you, Mrs. Magpie, I don't want any interference between my husband and me, and I will not have it," says Mrs. Oriole, with her little round eyes flashing with indignation.

"Don't put yourself in a passion, my dear; the more you talk, the more sure I am that your nervous system is running down, or you would n't forget good manners in this way. You 'd better take my advice, for I understand just what to do," — and away sails Mother Magpie; and presently young Oriole comes home, all in a flutter.

"I say, my dear, if you will persist in gossiping over our private family matters with that old Mother Magpie —"

"My dear, I don't gossip; she comes and bores me to death with talking, and then goes off and mistakes what she has been saying for what I said."

"But you must *cut* her."

"I try to, all I can; but she won't *be* cut.

"It 's enough to make a bird swear," said Tommy Oriole.

Tommy Oriole, to say the truth, had as good a heart as ever beat under bird's feathers; but then he had a weakness for concerts and general society, because he was held to be, by all odds, the handsomest bird in the woods, and sung like an angel; and so the truth was he did n't confine himself so much to the domestic nest as Tom Titmouse or Billy Wren. But he determined that he would n't have old Mother Magpie interfering with his affairs.

"The fact is," quoth Tommy, "I am a society bird, and Nature has marked out for me a course beyond the range of the commonplace, and my wife must learn to accommodate. If she has a brilliant husband, whose success gratifies her ambition and places her in a distinguished public position, she must pay something for it. I 'm sure Billy Wren's wife would give her very bill to see her husband in the circles where I am quite at home. To say the truth, my wife was all well enough content till old Mother Magpie interfered. It is quite my duty to take strong ground, and show that I cannot be dictated to."

So, after this, Tommy Oriole went to rather more concerts, and spent less time at home than ever he did before, which was all that Mother Magpie effected in that quarter. I confess this was very bad in Tommy; but then birds are no better than men in domestic matters, and sometimes will take the most unreasonable courses, if a meddlesome Magpie gets her claw into their nest.

But old Mother Magpie had now got a new business in hand in another quarter. She bustled off down to Waterdock Lane, where, as we said in a former narrative, lived

the old music-teacher, Dr. Bullfrog. The poor old Doctor
was a simple-minded, good, amiable creature, who had played
the double-bass and led the forest choir on all public occasions since nobody knows when. Latterly some youngsters
had arisen who sneered at his performances as behind the
age. In fact, since a great city had grown up in the vicinity
of the forest, tribes of wandering boys broke up the simple
tastes and quiet habits which old Mother Nature had always
kept up in those parts. They pulled the young checkerberry before it even had time to blossom, rooted up the
sassafras shrubs and gnawed their roots, fired off guns at
the birds, and, on several occasions when old Dr. Bullfrog
was leading a concert, had dashed in and broken up the
choir by throwing stones.

This was not the worst of it. The little varlets had a
way of jeering at the simple old Doctor and his concerts,
and mimicking the tones of his bass-viol. "There you go,
Paddy-go-donk, Paddy-go-donk — umph — chunk," some rascal of a boy would shout, while poor old Bullfrog's yellow
spectacles would be bedewed with tears of honest indignation.
In time, the jeers of these little savages began to tell on
the society in the forest, and to corrupt their simple manners ; and it was whispered among the younger and more
heavy birds and squirrels, that old Bullfrog was a bore, and
that it was time to get up a new style of music in the
parish, and to give the charge of it to some more modern
performer.

Poor old Dr. Bullfrog knew nothing of this, however, and was doing his simple best, in peace, when Mother Magpie called in upon him, one morning.

"Well, neighbor, how unreasonable people are! Who would have thought that the youth of our generation should have no more consideration for established merit? Now, for my part, *I* think your music-teaching never was better; and as for our choir, I maintain constantly that it never was in better order, but — Well, one may wear her tongue out, but one can never make these young folks listen to reason."

"I really don't understand you, ma'am," said poor Dr. Bullfrog.

"What! you have n't heard of a committee that is going to call on you, to ask you to resign the care of the parish music?"

"Madam," said Dr. Bullfrog, with all that energy of tone for which he was remarkable, "I don't believe it, — I *can't* believe it. You must have made a mistake."

"I mistake! No, no, my good friend; I never make mistakes. What I know, I know certainly. Was n't it I that said I knew there was an engagement between Tim Chipmunk and Nancy Nibble, who are married this blessed day? I knew that thing six weeks before any bird or beast in our parts; and I can tell you, you are going to be scandalously and ungratefully treated, Dr. Bullfrog."

"Bless me, we shall all be ruined!" said Mrs. Bullfrog; "my poor husband —"

"O, as to that, if you take things in time, and listen to my advice," said Mother Magpie, "we may yet pull you through. You must alter your style a little, — adapt it to modern times. Everybody now is a little touched with the operatic fever, and there 's Tommy Oriole has been to New Orleans and brought back a touch of the artistic. If you would try his style a little, — something Tyrolean, you see."

"Dear madam, consider my voice. I never could hit the high notes."

"How do you know? It's all practice; Tommy Oriole says so. Just try the scales. As to your voice, your manner of living has a great deal to do with it. I always did tell you that your passion for water injured your singing. Suppose Tommy Oriole should sit half his days up to his hips in water, as you do, — his voice would be as hoarse and rough as yours. Come up on the bank, and learn to perch, as we birds do. We are the true musical race."

And so, poor Mr. Bullfrog was persuaded to forego his pleasant little cottage under the cat-tails, where his green spectacles and honest round back had excited, even in the minds of the boys, sentiments of respect and compassion. He came up into the garden, and established himself under a burdock, and began to practise Italian scales.

The result was, that poor old Dr. Bullfrog, instead of being considered as a respectable old bore, got himself universally laughed at for aping fashionable manners. Every bird and beast in the forest had a gibe at him; and even old Parson Too-Whit thought it worth his while to make him a pastoral call, and admonish him about courses unbefitting his age and standing. As to Mother Magpie, you may be sure that she assured every one how sorry she was that dear old Dr. Bullfrog had made such a fool of himself; if he had taken her advice, he would have kept on respectably as a nice old Bullfrog should.

But the tragedy for the poor old music-teacher grew even

more melancholy in its termination ; for one day as he was
sitting disconsolately under a currant-bush in the garden,
practising his poor old notes in a quiet way, *thump* came
a great blow of a hoe, which nearly broke his back.

"Hullo! what ugly beast have we got here?" said Tom
Noakes, the gardener's boy. "Here, here, Wasp, my boy."

What a fright for a poor, quiet, old Bullfrog, as little
wiry, wicked Wasp came at him, barking and yelping. He
jumped with all his force sheer over a patch of bushes into
the river, and swam back to his old home among the cat-
tails. And always after that it was observable that he was
very low-spirited, and took very dark views of life ; but
nothing made him so angry as any allusion to Mother
Magpie, of whom, from that time, he never spoke except
as *Old Mother Mischief*.

THE SQUIRRELS THAT LIVE IN A HOUSE.

ONCE upon a time a gentleman went out into a great forest, and cut away the trees, and built there a very nice little cottage. It was set very low on the ground, and had very large bow-windows, and so much of it was glass that one could look through it on every side and see what was going on in the forest. You could see the shadows of the fern-leaves, as they flickered and wavered over the ground, and the scarlet partridge-berry and wintergreen plums that matted round the roots of the trees, and the bright spots of sunshine that fell through their branches and went dancing about among the bushes and leaves at their roots. You could see the little chipping sparrows and thrushes and robins and bluebirds building their nests here and there among the branches, and watch them from day to day as they laid their eggs and hatched their young. You could also see red squirrels, and gray squirrels, and little striped chip-squirrels, darting and springing about, here and there and everywhere, running races with each other from bough to bough, and chattering at each other in the gayest possible manner.

You may be sure that such a strange thing as a great mortal house for human beings to live in did not come into this wild wood without making quite a stir and excitement among the inhabitants that lived there before. All the time it was building, there was the greatest possible commotion in the breasts of all the older population; and there was n't even a black ant, or a cricket, that did not have his own opinion about it, and did not tell the other ants and crickets just what he thought the world was coming to in consequence.

Old Mrs. Rabbit declared that the hammering and pounding made her nervous, and gave her most melancholy forebodings of evil times. "Depend upon it, children," she said to her long-eared family, "no good will come to us from this establishment. Where man is, there comes always trouble for us poor rabbits."

The old chestnut-tree, that grew on the edge of the woodland ravine, drew a great sigh which shook all his leaves, and expressed it as his conviction that no good would ever come of it, — a conviction that at once struck to the heart of every chestnut-burr. The squirrels talked together of the dreadful state of things that would ensue. "Why!" said old Father Gray, "it's evident that Nature made the nuts for us; but one of these great human creatures will carry off and gormandize upon what would keep a hundred poor families of squirrels in comfort." Old Ground-mole said it did not require very sharp eyes to see into the future, and it would just end in bringing down the price of real estate in the whole vicinity, so that every decent-minded and respectable quadruped would be obliged to move away;—for his part, he was ready to sell out for anything he could get. The bluebirds and bobolinks, it is true, took more cheerful views of matters; but then, as old Mrs. Ground-mole observed, they were a flighty set,—half their time careering and dissipating in the Southern States, —and could not be expected to have that patriotic attachment to their native soil that those had who had grubbed in it from their earliest days.

"This race of man," said the old chestnut-tree, "is never ceasing in its restless warfare on Nature. In our forest solitudes, hitherto, how peacefully, how quietly, how regularly has everything gone on! Not a flower has missed its appointed time of blossoming, or failed to perfect its fruit. No matter how hard has been the winter, how loud the winds have roared, and how high the snow-banks have been piled, all has come right again in spring. Not the least root has lost itself under the snows, so as not to be ready with its fresh leaves and blossoms when the sun returns to melt the frosty chains of winter. We have storms sometimes that threaten to shake everything to pieces,—the thunder roars, the lightning flashes, and the winds howl and beat; but, when all is past, everything comes out better and brighter than before,—not a bird is killed, not the frailest flower destroyed. But man comes,

and in one day he will make a desolation that centuries
cannot repair. Ignorant boor that he is, and all incapable
of appreciating the glorious works of Nature, it seems to
be his glory to be able to destroy in a few hours what it
was the work of ages to produce. The noble oak, that has
been cut away to build this contemptible human dwelling,
had a life older and wiser than that of any man in this
country. That tree has seen generations of men come and
go. It was a fresh young tree when Shakespeare was
born ; it was hardly a middle-aged tree when he died ; it
was growing here when the first ship brought the white
men to our shores, and hundreds and hundreds of those
whom they call bravest, wisest, strongest, — warriors, states-
men, orators, and poets, — have been born, have grown up,
lived, and died, while yet it has outlived them all. It has
seen more wisdom than the best of them ; but two or three
hours of brutal strength sufficed to lay it low. Which of
these dolts could make a tree ? I 'd like to see them do
anything like it. How noisy and clumsy are all their movements, — chopping, pounding, rasping, hammering ! And,
after all, what do they build ? In the forest we do everything so quietly. A tree would be ashamed of itself that
could not get its growth without making such a noise and
dust and fuss. Our life is the perfection of good manners.
For my part, I feel degraded at the mere presence of these
human beings ; but, alas ! I am old ; — a hollow place at

my heart warns me of the progress of decay, and probably it will be seized upon by these rapacious creatures as an excuse for laying me as low as my noble green brother."

In spite of all this disquiet about it, the little cottage grew and was finished. The walls were covered with pretty paper, the floors carpeted with pretty carpets; and, in fact, when it was all arranged, and the garden walks laid out, and beds of flowers planted around, it began to be confessed, even among the most critical, that it was not after all so bad a thing as was to have been feared.

A black ant went in one day and made a tour of exploration up and down, over chairs and tables, up the ceilings and down again, and, coming out, wrote an article for the Crickets' Gazette, in which he described the new abode as a veritable palace. Several butterflies fluttered in and sailed about and were wonderfully delighted, and then a bumble-bee and two or three honey-bees, who expressed themselves well pleased with the house, but more especially enchanted with the garden. In fact, when it was found that the proprietors were very fond of the rural solitudes of Nature, and had come out there for the purpose of enjoying them undisturbed, — that they watched and spared the anemones, and the violets, and bloodroots, and dog's-tooth violets, and little woolly rolls of fern that began to grow up under the trees in spring, — that they never allowed a gun to be fired to scare the birds, and watched the building of their nests with the greatest interest, — then an opinion in favor of human beings began to gain ground, and every cricket and bird and beast was loud in their praise.

"Mamma," said young Tit-bit, a frisky young squirrel, to his mother one day, "why won't you let Frisky and me go into that pretty new cottage to play?"

"My dear," said his mother, who was a very wary and careful old squirrel, "how can you think of it? The race of man are full of devices for traps and pitfalls, and who could say what might happen, if you put yourself in their power? If you had wings like the butterflies and bees, you might fly in and out again, and so gratify your curiosity; but, as matters stand, it's best for you to keep well out of their way."

"But mother, there is such a nice, good lady lives there! I believe she is a good fairy, and she seems to love us all so; she sits in the bow-window and watches us for hours, and she scatters corn all round at the roots of the tree for us to eat."

"She is nice enough," said the old mother-squirrel, "if you keep far enough off; but I tell you, you can't be too careful."

Now this good fairy that the squirrels discoursed about was a nice little old lady that the children used to call Aunt Esther, and she was a dear lover of birds and squirrels, and all sorts of animals, and had studied their little ways till she knew just what would please them; and so she would every day throw out crumbs for the sparrows, and little bits of bread and wool and cotton to help the birds that were building their nests, and would scatter corn and nuts for the squirrels; and while she sat at her work in the bow-window she would smile to see the birds flying away with the wool, and the squirrels nibbling their nuts.   After a while the birds grew so tame that they would hop into the bow-window, and eat their crumbs off the carpet.

"There, mamma," said Tit-bit and Frisky, "only see! Jenny Wren and Cock Robin have been in at the bow-window, and it didn't hurt them, and why can't we go?"

"Well, my dears," said old Mother Squirrel, "you must do it very carefully: never forget that you haven't wings like Jenny Wren and Cock Robin."

So the next day Aunt Esther laid a train of corn from the roots of the trees to the bow-window, and then from the bow-window to her work-basket, which stood on the floor beside her; and then she put quite a handful of corn in the work-basket, and sat down by it, and seemed intent on her sewing.   Very soon, creep, creep, creep, came Tit-bit and Frisky to the window, and then into the room, just as sly and as still as could be, and Aunt Esther sat just like a statue for fear of disturbing them.

They looked all around in high glee, and when they came
to the basket it seemed to them a wonderful little summer-
house, made on purpose for them to play in.   They nosed
about in it, and turned over the scissors and the needle-
book, and took a nibble at her white wax, and jostled the
spools, meanwhile stowing away the corn each side of their
little chops, till they both of them looked as if they had
the mumps.

At last Aunt Esther put out her hand to touch them,
when, whisk-frisk, out they went, and up the trees, chattering and laughing before she had time even to wink.

But after this they used to come in every day, and when
she put corn in her hand and held it very still they would
eat out of it; and, finally, they would get into her hand,
until one day she gently closed it over them, and Frisky
and Tit-bit were fairly caught.

O, how their hearts beat! but the good fairy only spoke
gently to them, and soon unclosed her hand and let them
go again.   So, day after day, they grew to have more and
more faith in her, till they would climb into her work-basket,
sit on her shoulder, or nestle away in her lap as she sat
sewing.   They made also long exploring voyages all over the
house, up and through all the chambers, till finally, I grieve
to say, poor Frisky came to an untimely end by being
drowned in the water-tank at the top of the house.

The dear good fairy passed away from the house in time,

and went to a land where the flowers never fade, and the birds never die; but the squirrels still continue to make the place a favorite resort.

"In fact, my dear," said old Mother Red one winter to her mate, "what is the use of one's living in this cold, hollow tree, when these amiable people have erected this pretty cottage where there is plenty of room for us and them too? Now I have examined between the eaves, and there is a charming place where we can store our nuts, and where we can whip in and out of the garret, and have the free range of the house; and, say what you will, these humans

5

have delightful ways of being warm and comfortable in winter."

So Mr. and Mrs. Red set up housekeeping in the cottage, and had no end of nuts and other good things stored up there. The trouble of all this was, that, as Mrs. Red was a notable body, and got up to begin her housekeeping operations, and woke up all her children, at four o'clock in the morning, the good people often were disturbed by a great rattling and fuss in the walls, while yet it seemed dark night. Then sometimes, too, I grieve to say, Mrs. Squirrel would give her husband vigorous curtain lectures in the night, which made him so indignant that he would rattle off to another quarter of the garret to sleep by himself; and all this broke the rest of the worthy people who built the house.

What is to be done about this we don't know. What would you do about it? Would you let the squirrels live in your house, or not? When our good people come down of a cold winter morning, and see the squirrels dancing and frisking down the trees, and chasing each other so merrily over the garden-chair between them, or sitting with their tails saucily over their backs, they look so jolly and jaunty and pretty that they almost forgive them for disturbing their night's rest, and think that they will not do anything to drive them out of the garret to-day. And so it goes on ; but how long the squirrels will rent the cottage in this fashion, I 'm sure I dare not undertake to say.

HUM, THE SON OF BUZ.

AT Rye Beach, during our summer's vacation, there came, as there always will to seaside visitors, two or three cold, chilly, rainy days, — days when the skies that long had not rained a drop seemed suddenly to bethink themselves of their remissness, and to pour down water, not by drops, but by pailfuls. The chilly wind blew and whistled, the water dashed along the ground, and careered in foamy rills along the roadside, and the bushes bent beneath the constant flood. It was plain that there was to be no sea-bathing on such a day, no walks, no rides; and so, shivering and drawing our blanket-shawls close about us, we sat down to the window to watch the storm outside. The rose-bushes under the window hung dripping under their load of moisture, each spray shedding a constant shower on the spray below it. On one of these lower sprays, under the perpetual drip, what should we see but a poor little humming-bird, drawn up into the tiniest shivering ball, and clinging with a desperate grasp to his uncomfortable perch. A humming-bird we knew him to be at once, though his feathers were so matted and glued down by the rain that he looked not much bigger than a honey-bee, and as different as possible from the

smart, pert, airy little character that we had so often seen
flirting with the flowers.   He was evidently a humming-
bird in adversity, and whether he ever would hum again
looked to us exceedingly doubtful.   Immediately, however,
we sent out to have him taken in.   When the friendly
hand seized him, he gave a little, faint, watery squeak, evidently thinking that his last hour was come, and that grim
Death was about to carry him off to the land of dead
birds.   What a time we had reviving him, — holding the
little wet thing in the warm hollow of our hands, and
feeling him shiver and palpitate !   His eyes were fast
closed ; his tiny claws, which looked slender as cobwebs,
were knotted close to his body, and it was long before one
could feel the least motion in them.   Finally, to our great
joy, we felt a brisk little kick, and then a flutter of wings,
and then a determined peck of the beak, which showed
that there was some bird left in him yet, and that he
meant at any rate to find out where he was.

Unclosing our hands a small space, out popped the li:·
tle head with a pair of round brilliant eyes.   Then we
bethought ourselves of feeding him, and forthwith prepared
him a stiff glass of sugar and water, a drop of which we
held to his bill.   After turning his head attentively, like
a bird who knew what he was about and did n't mean to
be chaffed, he briskly put out a long, flexible tongue,
slightly forked at the end, and licked off the comfortable

beverage with great relish. Immediately he was pronounced
out of danger by the small humane society which had un-
dertaken the charge of his restoration, and we began to
cast about for getting him a settled establishment in our
apartment. I gave up my work-box to him for a sleeping-
room, and it was medically ordered that he should take
a nap. So we filled the box with cotton, and he was
formally put to bed with a folded cambric handkerchief
round his neck, to keep him from beating his wings. Out
of his white wrappings he looked forth green and grave
as any judge with his bright round eyes. Like a bird of
discretion, he seemed to understand what was being done
to him, and resigned himself sensibly to go to sleep.

The box was covered with a sheet of paper perforated
with holes for purposes of ventilation; for even humming-
birds have a little pair of lungs, and need their own little
portion of air to fill them, so that they may make bright
scarlet little drops of blood to keep life's fire burning in
their tiny bodies. Our bird's lungs manufactured brilliant blood, as we found out by experience; for in his
first nap he contrived to nestle himself into the cotton of
which his bed was made, and to get more of it than he
needed into his long bill. We pulled it out as carefully
as we could, but there came out of his bill two round,
bright, scarlet, little drops of blood. Our chief medical
authority looked grave, pronounced a probable hemor-

rhage from the lungs, and gave him over at once. We, less scientific, declared that we had only cut his little tongue by drawing out the filaments of cotton, and that he would do well enough in time, — as it afterward appeared he did, — for from that day there was no more bleeding. In the course of the second day he began to take short flights about the room, though he seemed to prefer to return to us, — perching on our fingers or heads or shoulders, and sometimes choosing to sit in this way for half an hour at a time. "These great giants," he seemed to say to himself, "are not bad people after all; they have a comfortable way with them; how nicely they dried and warmed me! Truly a bird might do worse than to live with them."

So he made up his mind to form a fourth in the little company of three that usually sat and read, worked and sketched, in that apartment, and we christened him "Hum, the son of Buz." He became an individuality, a character, whose little doings formed a part of every letter, and some extracts from these will show what some of his little ways were.

"Hum has learned to sit upon my finger, and eat his sugar and water out of a teaspoon with most Christian-like decorum. He has but one weakness, — he will occasionally jump into the spoon and sit in his sugar and water, and then appear to wonder where it goes to. His plumage is in rather a drabbled state, owing to these performances. I have sketched him as he sat to-day on a bit of Spiræa which I brought in for him. When absorbed in reflection, he sits with his bill straight up in the air, as I have drawn him. Mr. A—— reads Macaulay to us, and you should see the wise air with which, perched on Jenny's thumb, he cocked his head now one side and then the other, apparently listening with most critical attention. His confidence in us seems unbounded ; he lets us stroke his head, smooth his feathers, without a flutter ; and is never better pleased than sitting, as he has been doing all this while, on my hand, turning up his bill, and watching my face with great edification.

"I have just been having a sort of maternal struggle to make him go to bed in his box; but he evidently considers himself sufficiently convalescent to make a stand for his rights as a bird, and so scratched indignantly out of his wrappings, and set himself up to roost on the edge of the box, with an air worthy of a turkey, at the very least. Having brought in a lamp, he has opened his eyes round and wide, and sits cocking his little head at me reflectively."

When the weather cleared away, and the sun came out bright, Hum became entirely well, and seemed resolved to take the measure of his new life with us. Our windows were closed in the lower part of the sash by frames with mosquito gauze, so that the sun and air found free admission, and yet our little rover could not pass out. On the first sunny day he took an exact survey of our apartment from ceiling to floor, humming about, examining every point with his bill, — all the crevices, mouldings, each little indentation in the bed-posts, each window-pane, each chair and stand; and, as it was a very simply furnished seaside apartment, his scrutiny was soon finished. We wondered, at first, what this was all about; but, on watching him more closely, we found that he was actively engaged in getting his living, by darting out his long tongue hither and thither, and drawing in all the tiny flies and insects which in summer-time are to be found in an apartment. In short, we found that, though the nectar of flowers was his dessert, yet he had his roast beef and mutton-chop to look after, and that his bright, brilliant blood was not made out of a simple vegetarian diet. Very shrewd and keen he was, too, in measuring the size of insects before he attempted to swallow them. The smallest class were whisked off with lightning speed; but about larger ones he would sometimes wheel and hum for some minutes, darting hither and thither, and surveying them warily; and if satisfied that they could be carried, he would come down with a quick, central dart which would finish the unfortunate at a snap. The larger flies seemed to irritate him, — especially when they intimated to him that his plumage was sugary, by settling on his wings and tail; when he would lay about him spitefully, wielding his bill like a sword. A grasshopper that strayed in, and was sunning himself on the window-seat, gave him great discomposure. Hum evidently considered him an intruder, and seemed to long to make a dive at him; but, with characteristic prudence, confined himself to threatening movements, which did not exactly hit. He saw evidently that he could not swallow him whole, and what might ensue from trying him piecemeal he wisely forbore to essay.

Hum had his own favorite places and perches. From the first day he chose for his nightly roost a towel-line which had been drawn across the corner over the wash-stand, where he every night established himself with one claw in the edge of the towel and the other clasping the line, and, ruffling up his feathers till he looked like a little chestnut-burr, he would resign himself to the soundest sleep. He did not tuck his head under his wing, but seemed to sink it down between his shoulders, with his bill almost straight up in the air. One evening one of us, going to use the towel, jarred the line, and soon after found that Hum had been thrown from his perch, and was hanging head downward, fast asleep, still clinging to the line. Another evening, being discomposed by somebody coming to the towel-line after he had settled himself, he fluttered off; but so sleepy that he had not discretion to poise himself

again, and was found clinging, like a little bunch of green
floss silk, to the mosquito netting of the window.

A day after this we brought in a large green bough, and
put it up over the looking-glass. Hum noticed it before it
had been there five minutes, flew to it, and began a regular survey, perching now here, now there, till he seemed to
find a twig that exactly suited him; and after that he
roosted there every night. Who does not see in this
change all the signs of reflection and reason that are
shown by us in thinking over our circumstances, and trying to better them? It seemed to say in so many words:
"That towel-line is an unsafe place for a bird; I get
frightened, and wake from bad dreams to find myself head
downwards; so I will find a better roost on this twig."

When our little Jenny one day put on a clean white
muslin gown embellished with red sprigs, Hum flew towards
her, and with his bill made instant examination of these
new appearances; and one day, being very affectionately
disposed, perched himself on her shoulder, and sat some
time. On another occasion, while Mr. A—— was reading,
Hum established himself on the top of his head just over
the middle of his forehead, in the precise place where our
young belles have lately worn stuffed humming-birds, making him look as if dressed out for a party. Hum's most
favorite perch was the back of the great rocking-chair, which,
being covered by a tidy, gave some hold into which he

could catch his little claws. There he would sit, balancing himself cleverly if its occupant chose to swing to and fro, and seeming to be listening to the conversation or reading.

Hum had his different moods, like human beings. On cold, cloudy, gray days he appeared to be somewhat depressed in spirits, hummed less about the room, and sat humped up with his feathers ruffled, looking as much like a bird in a great-coat as possible. But on hot, sunny days, every feather sleeked itself down, and his little body looked natty and trim, his head alert, his eyes bright, and it was impossible to come near him, for his agility. Then let mosquitoes and little flies look about them! Hum snapped them up without mercy, and seemed to be all over the ceiling in a moment, and resisted all our efforts at any personal familiarity with a saucy alacrity.

Hum had his established institutions in our room, the chief of which was a tumbler with a little sugar and water mixed in it, and a spoon laid across, out of which he helped himself whenever he felt in the mood, — sitting on the edge of the tumbler, and dipping his long bill, and lapping with his little forked tongue like a kitten. When he found his spoon accidentally dry, he would stoop over and dip his bill in the water in the tumbler, — which caused the prophecy on the part of some of his guardians, that he would fall in some day and be drowned. For which reason it was agreed to keep only an inch in depth of the fluid at the

bottom of the tumbler. A wise precaution this proved; for the next morning I was awaked, not by the usual hum over my head, but by a sharp little flutter, and found Mr. Hum beating his wings in the tumbler, — having actually tumbled in during his energetic efforts to get his morning coffee before I was awake.

Hum seemed perfectly happy and satisfied in his quarters, — but one day, when the door was left open, made a dart out, and so into the open sunshine. Then, to be sure, we thought we had lost him. We took the mosquito netting

out of all the windows, and, setting his tumbler of sugar
and water in a conspicuous place, went about our usual
occupations. We saw him joyous and brisk among the
honeysuckles outside the window, and it was gravely predicted that he would return no more. But at dinner-time
in came Hum, familiar as possible, and sat down to his
spoon as if nothing had happened ; instantly we closed our
windows and had him secure once more.

At another time I was going to ride to the Atlantic
House, about a mile from my boarding-place. I left all
secure, as I supposed, at home. While gathering moss on
the walls there, I was surprised by a little green humming-
bird flying familiarly right towards my face, and humming
above my head. I called out, "Here is Hum's very brother."
But, on returning home, I saw that the door of the room
was open, and Hum was gone. Now certainly we gave
him up for lost. I sat down to painting, and in a few
minutes in flew Hum, and settled on the edge of my tumbler in a social, confidential way, which seemed to say, "O,
you 've got back then." After taking his usual drink of
sugar and water, he began to fly about the ceiling as usual,
and we gladly shut him in.

When our five weeks at the seaside were up, and it was
time to go home, we had great questionings what was to
be done with Hum. To get him home with us was our
desire, — but who ever heard of a humming-bird travelling

by railroad? Great were the consultings; a little basket of Indian work was filled up with cambric handkerchiefs, and a bottle of sugar and water provided, and we started with him for a day's journey. When we arrived at night the first care was to see what had become of Hum, who had not been looked at since we fed him with sugar and water in Boston. We found him alive and well, but so dead asleep that we could not wake him to roost; so we put him to bed on a toilet cushion, and arranged his tumbler for morning. The next day found him alive and humming, exploring the room and pictures, perching now here and now there; but, as the weather was chilly, he sat for the most part of the time in a humped-up state on the tip of a pair of stag's horns. We moved him to a more sunny apartment; but, alas! the equinoctial storm came on, and there was no sun to be had for days. Hum was blue; the pleasant seaside days were over; his room was lonely, the pleasant three that had enlivened the apartment at Rye no longer came in and out; evidently he was lonesome, and gave way to depression. One chilly morning he managed again to fall into his tumbler, and wet himself through; and notwithstanding warm bathings and tender nursings, the poor little fellow seemed to get diphtheria, or something quite as bad for humming-birds.

We carried him to a neighboring sunny parlor, where ivy embowers all the walls, and the sun lies all day. There he

revived a little, danced up and down, perched on a green
spray that was wreathed across the breast of a Psyche, and
looked then like a little flitting soul returning to its rest.
Towards evening he drooped ; and, having been nursed and
warmed and cared for, he was put to sleep on a green
twig laid on the piano. In that sleep the little head drooped
— nodded — fell ; and little Hum went where other bright
dreams go, — to the Land of the Hereafter.

OUR COUNTRY NEIGHBORS.

WE have just built our house in rather an out-of-the-way place, — on the bank of a river, and under the shade of a patch of woods which is a veritable remain of quite an ancient forest. The checkerberry and partridge-plum, with their glossy green leaves and scarlet berries, still carpet the ground under its deep shadows; and prince's-pine and other kindred evergreens declare its native wildness, — for these are children of the wild woods, that never come after plough and harrow has once broken a soil.

When we tried to look out the spot for our house, we had to get a surveyor to go before us and cut a path through the dense underbrush that was laced together in a general network of boughs and leaves, and grew so high as to overtop our heads. Where the house stands, four or five great old oaks and chestnuts had to be cut away to let it in; and now it stands on the bank of the river, the edges of which are still overhung with old forest-trees, chestnuts and oaks, which look at themselves in the glassy stream.

A little knoll near the house was chosen for a garden-spot; a dense, dark mass of trees above, of bushes in mid-air, and of all sorts of ferns and wild-flowers and creeping vines on the ground. All these had to be cleared out, and a dozen great trees cut down and dragged off to a neighboring saw-mill, there to be transformed into boards to finish off our house. Then, fetching a great machine, such as might be used to pull a giant's teeth, with ropes, pulleys, oxen, and men, and might and main, we pulled out the stumps, with their great prongs and their network of roots and fibres; and then, alas! we had to begin with all the pretty wild, lovely bushes, and the checkerberries and ferns and wild blackberries and huckleberry-bushes, and dig them up remorselessly, that we might plant our corn and squashes. And so we got a house and a garden right out of the heart of our piece of wild wood, about a mile from the city of H——.

Well, then, people said it was a lonely place, and far from neighbors, — by which they meant that it was a good way for them to come to see us. But we soon found that whoever goes into the woods to live finds neighbors of a new kind, and some to whom it is rather hard to become accustomed.

For instance, on a fine day early in April, as we were crossing over to superintend the building of our house, we were startled by a striped snake, with his little bright eyes, raising himself to look at us, and putting out his red, forked tongue. Now there is no more harm in these little

6

garden-snakes than there is in a robin or a squirrel; they are poor little, peaceable, timid creatures, which could not do any harm if they would; but the prejudices of society are so strong against them, that one does not like to cultivate too much intimacy with them. So we tried to turn out of our path into a tangle of bushes; and there, instead of one, we found four snakes. We turned on the other side, and there were two more. In short, everywhere we looked, the dry leaves were rustling and coiling with them; and we were in despair. In vain we said that they were harmless as kittens, and tried to persuade ourselves that their little bright eyes were pretty, and that their serpentine movements were in the exact line of beauty; for the life of us, we could not help remembering their family name and connections; we thought of those disagreeable gentlemen, the anacondas, the rattlesnakes, and the copperheads, and all of that bad line, immediate family friends of the old serpent to whom we are indebted for all the mischief that is done in this world. So we were quite apprehensive when we saw how our new neighborhood was infested by them, until a neighbor calmed out fears by telling us that snakes always crawled out of their holes to sun themselves in the spring, and that in a day or two they would all be gone.

So it proved. It was evident they were all out merely to do their spring shopping, or something that serves with them the same purpose that spring shopping does with us; and where they went afterwards we do not know. People speak of snakes' holes, and we have seen them disappearing into such subterranean chambers; but we never opened one to see what sort of underground housekeeping went on there. After the first few days of spring, a snake was a rare visitor, though now and then one appeared.

One was discovered taking his noontide repast one day in a manner which excited much prejudice. He was, in fact, regaling himself by sucking down into his maw a small frog, which he had begun to swallow at the toes, and had drawn about half down. The frog, it must be confessed, seemed to view this arrangement with great indifference, making no struggle, and sitting solemnly, with his great unwinking eyes, to be sucked in at the leisure of his captor. There was immense sympathy, however, excited for him in the family circle; and it was voted that a snake which indulged in such very disagreeable modes of eating his dinner was not to be tolerated in our vicinity. So I have reason to believe that that was his last meal.

Another of our wild woodland neighbors made us some trouble. It was no other than a veritable woodchuck, whose hole we had often wondered at when we were scrambling through the underbrush after spring flowers. The hole was about the size of a peck-measure, and had two openings about six feet apart. The occupant was a gentleman we never had had the pleasure of seeing; but we soon learned his existence from his ravages in our garden. He had a taste, it appears, for the very kind of things we wanted to eat ourselves, and helped himself without asking. We had a row of fine, crisp heads of lettuce, which were the pride of our gardening, and out of which he would from day to day select for his table just the plants we had marked for ours. He also nibbled our young beans; and so at last we were reluctantly obliged to let John Gardiner set a trap for him. Poor old simple-minded hermit, he was too artless for this world! He was caught at the very first snap, and found dead in the trap, — the agitation and distress having broken his poor woodland heart, and killed him. We were grieved to the very soul when the poor fat old fellow was dragged out, with his useless paws standing up stiff and imploring. As it was, he was given to Denis, our pig, which, without a single scruple of delicacy, ate him up as thoroughly as he ate up the lettuce.

This business of eating, it appears, must go on all through creation. We eat ducks, turkeys, and chickens, though we don't swallow them whole, feathers and all. Our four-footed friends, less civilized, take things with more directness and simplicity, and chew each other up without ceremony, or swallow each other alive. Of these unceremonious habits we had other instances.

Our house had a central court on the southern side, into which looked the library, dining-room, and front hall, as well as several of the upper chambers. It was designed to be closed in with glass, to serve as a conservatory in winter; and meanwhile we had filled it with splendid plumy ferns, taken up out of the neighboring wood. In the centre was a fountain surrounded by stones, shells, mosses, and various water-plants. We had bought three little goldfish to swim in our basin; and the spray of it, as it rose in the air and rippled back into the water, was the pleasantest possible sound of a hot day. We used to lie on the sofa in the hall, and look into the court, and fancy we saw some scene of fairy-land, and water-sprites coming up from the fountain. Suddenly a new-comer presented himself, — no other than an immense bullfrog, that had hopped up from the neighboring river, apparently with a view to making a permanent settlement in and about our fountain. He was to be seen, often for hours, sitting reflectively on the edge of it, beneath the broad shadow of the calla-leaves. When sometimes missed thence, he would be found under the ample shield of a great bignonia, whose striped leaves grew hard by.

The family were prejudiced against him. What did he want there? It was surely some sinister motive impelled him. He was probably watching for an opportunity to gobble up the goldfish. We took his part, however, and

strenuously defended his moral character, and patronized
him in all ways. We gave him the name of Unke, and
maintained that he was a well-conducted, philosophical old
water-sprite, who showed his good taste in wanting to take
up his abode in our conservatory. We even defended his
personal appearance, praised the invisible-green coat which
he wore on his back, and his gray vest, and solemn gold

spectacles; and though he always felt remarkably slimy
when we touched him, yet, as he would sit still, and allow
us to stroke his head and pat his back, we concluded his
social feelings might be warm, notwithstanding a cold ex-
terior. Who knew, after all, but he might be a beautiful
young prince, enchanted there till the princess should come
to drop the golden ball into the fountain, and so give him
a chance to marry her, and turn into a man again? Such
things, we are credibly informed, are matters of frequent
occurrence in Germany. Why not here?

By and by there came to our fountain another visitor, —
a frisky, green young frog of the identical kind spoken of
by the poet : —

> " There was a frog lived in a well,
> Rig dum pully metakimo."

This thoughtless, dapper individual, with his bright green
coat, his faultless white vest, and sea-green tights, became
rather the popular favorite. He seemed just rakish and
gallant enough to fulfil the conditions of the song : —

> " The frog he would a courting ride,
> With sword and pistol by his side."

This lively young fellow, whom we shall Cri-Cri, like other
frisky and gay young people, carried the day quite over
the head of the solemn old philosopher under the calla-
leaves. At night, when all was still, he would trill a joy-

ous little note in his throat, while old Unke would answer only with a cracked guttural more singular than agreeable; and to all outward appearance the two were as good friends as their different natures would allow.

One day, however, the conservatory became a scene of a tragedy of the deepest dye. We were summoned below by shrieks and howls of horror. "Do pray come down and see what this vile, nasty, horrid old frog has been doing!" Down we came; and there sat our virtuous old philosopher, with his poor little brother's hind legs still sticking out of the corner of his mouth, as if he were smoking them for a cigar, all helplessly palpitating as they were. In fact, our solemn old friend had done what many a solemn hypocrite before has done, — swallowed his poor brother, neck and crop, — and sat there with the most brazen indifference, looking as if he had done the most proper and virtuous thing in the world.

Immediately he was marched out of the conservatory at the point of the walking-stick, and made to hop down into the river, into whose waters he splashed; and we saw him no more. We regret to say that the popular indignation was so precipitate in its results; otherwise the special artist who sketched Hum, the son of Buz, intended to have made a sketch of the old villain, as he sat with his luckless victim's hind legs projecting from his solemn mouth. With all his moral faults, he was a good sitter, and would probably have sat immovable any length of time that could be desired.

Of other woodland neighbors there were some which we saw occasionally. The shores of the river were lined here and there with the holes of the muskrats; and, in rowing by their settlements, we were sometimes strongly reminded of them by the overpowering odor of the perfume from which they get their name. There were also owls, whose nests were high up in some of the old chestnut-trees. Often in the lonely hours of the night we could hear them gibbering with a sort of wild, hollow laugh among the distant trees. But one tenant of the woods made us some trouble in the autumn. It was a little flying-squirrel, who took to making excursions into our house in the night season, coming down chimney into the chambers, rustling about among the clothes, cracking nuts or nibbling at any morsels of anything that suited his fancy. For a long time the inmates of the rooms were awakened in the night by mysterious noises, thumps, and rappings, and so lighted candles, and searched in vain to find whence they came; for the moment any movement was made, the rogue whipped up chimney, and left us a prey to the most mysterious alarms. What could it be?

But one night our fine gentleman bounced in at the window of another room, which had no fireplace; and the fair occupant, rising in the night, shut the window, without suspecting that she had cut off the retreat of any of her woodland neighbors. The next morning she was startled by what she thought a gray rat running past her bed. She rose to pursue him, when he ran up the wall, and clung against the plastering, showing himself very plainly a gray flying-squirrel, with large, soft eyes, and wings which consisted of a membrane uniting the fore paws to the hind ones, like those of a bat. He was chased into the conservatory, and, a window being opened, out he flew upon the ground, and made away for his native woods, and thus put an end to many fears as to the nature of our nocturnal rappings.

So you see how many neighbors we found by living in the woods, and, after all, no worse ones than are found in the great world.

OUR DOGS.

I.

WE who live in Cunopolis are a dog-loving family.
We have a warm side towards everything that goes
upon four paws, and the consequence has been that, taking
things first and last, we have been always kept in confusion and under the paw, so to speak, of some honest four-
footed tyrant, who would go beyond his privilege and
overrun the whole house. Years ago this begun, when
our household consisted of a papa, a mamma, and three
or four noisy boys and girls, and a kind Miss Anna who
acted as a second mamma to the whole. There was also
one more of our number, the youngest, dear little bright-
eyed Charley, who was king over us all, and rode in a
wicker wagon for a chariot, and had a nice little nurse
devoted to him; and it was through him that our first
dog came.

One day Charley's nurse took him quite a way to a
neighbor's house to spend the afternoon; and, he being
well amused, they stayed till after nightfall. The kind old
lady of the mansion was concerned that the little prince in
his little coach, with his little maid, had to travel so far in

the twilight shadows, and so she called a big dog named Carlo, and gave the establishment into his charge.

Carlo was a great, tawny-yellow mastiff, as big as a calf, with great, clear, honest eyes, and stiff, wiry hair; and the good lady called him to the side of the little wagon, and said, "Now, Carlo, you must take good care of Charley, and you must n't let anything hurt him."

Carlo wagged his tail in promise of protection, and away he trotted, home with the wicker wagon; and when he arrived, he was received with so much applause by four little folks, who dearly loved the very sight of a dog, he was so stroked and petted and caressed, that he concluded that he liked the place better than the home he came from, where were only very grave elderly people. He tarried all night, and slept at the foot of the boys' bed, who could hardly go to sleep for the things they found to say to him, and who were awake ever so early in the morning, stroking his rough, tawny back, and hugging him.

At his own home Carlo had a kennel all to himself, where he was expected to live quite alone, and do duty by watching and guarding the place. Nobody petted him, or stroked his rough hide, or said, "Poor dog!" to him, and so it appears he had a feeling that he was not appreciated, and liked our warm-hearted little folks, who told him stories, gave him half of their own supper, and took him to bed with them sociably. Carlo was a dog that had a mind of his own, though he could n't say much about it, and in his dog fashion proclaimed his likes and dislikes quite as strongly as if he could speak. When the time came for taking him home, he growled and showed his teeth dangerously at the man who was sent for him, and it was necessary to drag him back by force, and tie him into his kennel. However, he soon settled that matter by gnawing the rope in two and padding down again and appearing among his little friends, quite to their delight. Two or three times was he taken back and tied or chained; but he howled so dismally, and snapped at people in such a misanthropic manner, that finally the kind old lady thought it better to have no dog at all than a dog soured by blighted affection. So she loosed his rope, and said, "There, Carlo, go and stay where you like"; and so Carlo came to us, and a joy and delight was he to all in the house. He loved one and all; but he declared himself as more than all the slave and property of our little Prince Charley. He would lie on the floor as still as a door-mat, and let him pull his hair, and roll over him, and examine his eyes with his little fat fingers; and Carlo submitted to all these personal freedoms with as good an understanding as papa himself. When Charley slept, Carlo stretched himself along under the crib; rising now and then, and standing with his broad breast on a level with the slats of the crib, he would look down upon him with an air of grave pro-

tection. He also took a great fancy to papa, and would
sometimes pat with tiptoe care into his study, and sit
quietly down by him when he was busy over his Greek
or Latin books, waiting for a word or two of praise or en-
couragement. If none came, he would lay his rough horny
paw on his knee, and look in his face with such an honest, imploring expression, that the professor was forced to
break off to say, "Why, Carlo, you poor, good, honest
fellow,—did he want to be talked to?—so he did. Well,
he shall be talked to;—he 's a nice, good dog";—and
during all these praises Carlo's transports and the thumps
of his rough tail are not to be described.

He had great, honest yellowish-brown eyes, — not remarkable for their beauty, but which used to look as if he
longed to speak, and he seemed to have a yearning for

praise and love and caresses that even all our attentions
could scarcely satisfy. His master would say to him sometimes, "Carlo, you poor, good, homely dog, — how loving
you are !"

Carlo was a full-blooded mastiff, and his beauty, if he
had any, consisted in his having all the good points of his
race. He was a dog of blood, come of real old mastiff
lineage ; his stiff, wiry hair, his big, rough paws, and great
brawny chest, were all made for strength rather than beauty ;
but for all that he was a dog of tender sentiments. Yet,
if any one intruded on his rights and dignities, Carlo
showed that he had hot blood in him ; his lips would go
back, and show a glistening row of ivories, that one would
not like to encounter, and if any trenched on his privileges,
he would give a deep warning growl, — as much as to say,
"I am your slave for love, but you must treat me well, or
I shall be dangerous." A blow he would not bear from
any one : the fire would flash from his great yellow eyes,
and he would snap like a rifle ; — yet he would let his
own Prince Charley pound on his ribs with both baby
fists, and pull his tail till he yelped, without even a show
of resistance.

At last came a time when the merry voice of little Charley was heard no more, and his little feet no more pattered
through the halls ; he lay pale and silent in his little crib,
with his dear life ebbing away, and no one knew how to

stop its going. Poor old Carlo lay under the crib when they would let him, sometimes rising up to look in with an earnest, sorrowful face; and sometimes he would stretch himself out in the entry before the door of little Charley's room, watching with his great open eyes lest the thief should come in the night to steal away our treasure.

But one morning when the children woke, one little soul had gone in the night,— gone upward to the angels; and then the cold, pale little form that used to be the life of the house was laid away tenderly in the yard of a neighboring church.

Poor old Carlo would pit-pat silently about the house in those days of grief, looking first into one face and then another, but no one could tell him where his gay little master had gone. The other children had hid the baby-wagon away in the lumber-room lest their mamma should see it; and so passed a week or two, and Carlo saw no trace of Charley about the house. But then a lady in the neighborhood, who had a sick baby, sent to borrow the wicker wagon, and it was taken from its hiding-place to go to her. Carlo came to the door just as it was being drawn out of the gate into the street. Immediately he sprung, cleared the fence with a great bound, and ran after it. He overtook it, and poked his nose between the curtains,— there was no one there. Immediately he turned away, and padded dejectedly home. What words could have spoken plainer of love and memory than this one action ?

Carlo lived with us a year after this, when a time came for the whole family hive to be taken up and moved away from the flowery banks of the Ohio, to the piny shores of Maine. All our household goods were being uprooted, disordered, packed, and sold ; and the question daily arose, "What shall we do with Carlo ?" There was hard begging on the part of the boys that he might go with them, and one even volunteered to travel all the way in baggage cars to keep Carlo company. But papa said no, and so it was decided to send Carlo up the river to the home of a very genial lady who had visited in our family, and who appreciated his parts, and offered him a home in hers.

The matter was anxiously talked over one day in the family circle while Carlo lay under the table, and it was agreed that papa and Willie should take him to the steamboat landing the next morning. But the next morning Mr. Carlo was nowhere to be found. In vain was he called, from garret to cellar ; nor was it till papa and Willie had gone to the city that he came out of his hiding-place. For two or three days it was impossible to catch him, but after a while his suspicions were laid, and we learned not to speak out our plans in his presence, and so the transfer at last was prosperously effected.

We heard from him once in his new home, as being a

7

highly appreciated member of society, and adorning his new situation with all sorts of dog virtues, while we wended our ways to the coast of Maine. But our hearts were sore for want of him; the family circle seemed incomplete, until a new favorite appeared to take his place, of which I shall tell you next month.

II.

A NEIGHBOR, blessed with an extensive litter of Newfoundland pups, commenced one chapter in our family history by giving us a puppy, brisk, funny, and lively enough, who was received in our house with acclamations of joy, and christened "Rover." An auspicious name we all thought, for his four or five human playfellows were all rovers, — rovers in the woods, rovers by the banks of a neighboring patch of water, where they dashed and splashed, made rafts, inaugurated boats, and lived among the cat-tails and sweet flags as familiarly as so many muskrats. Rovers also they were, every few days, down to the shores of the great sea, where they caught fish, rowed boats, dug clams, — both girls and boys, — and one sex quite as handily as the other. Rover came into such a lively circle quite as one of them, and from the very first seemed to regard himself as part and parcel of all that was going on, in doors or out. But his exuberant spirits at times brought him into sad scrapes. His vivacity was such as to amount to decided insanity, — and mamma and Miss Anna and papa had many grave looks over his capers. Once he actually tore off the leg of a new pair of trousers that Johnny had just donned, and came racing home with it in his mouth, with its bare-legged little owner behind, screaming threats and maledictions on the robber. What a commotion! The new trousers had just been painfully finished, in those days when sewing was sewing, and not a mere jig on a sewing-machine; but Rover, so far from being abashed or ashamed, displayed an impish glee in his performance, bounding and leaping hither and thither with his trophy in his mouth, now growling and mangling it, and shaking it at us in elfish triumph as we chased him hither and thither, — over the wood-pile, into the woodhouse, through the barn, out of the stable door, — vowing all sorts of dreadful punishments when we caught him. But we might well say that, for the little wretch would never be caught; after one of his tricks, he always managed to keep himself out of arm's length till the thing was a little blown over, when in he would come, airy as ever, and wagging his little pudgy puppy tail with an air of the most perfect assurance in the world.

There is no saying what youthful errors were pardoned to him. Once he ate a hole in the bed-quilt as his night's employment, when one of the boys had surreptitiously got him into bed with them; he nibbled and variously maltreated sundry sheets; and once actually tore up and chewed off a corner of the bedroom carpet, to stay his stomach during the night season. What he did it for, no mortal knows; certainly it could not be because he was hungry, for there were five little pairs of hands incessantly feeding him from morning till night. Beside which, he had a boundless appetite for shoes, which he mumbled, and shook, and tore, and ruined, greatly to the vexation of their rightful owners, — rushing in and carrying them from the bedsides in the night-watches, racing off with them to any out-of-the-way corner that hit his fancy, and leaving them when he was tired of the fun. So there is no telling of the disgrace into which he brought his little masters and mistresses, and the tears and threats and scoldings which were all wasted on him, as he would stand quite at his ease, lolling out his red, saucy tongue, and never deigning to tell what he had done with his spoils.

Notwithstanding all these sins, Rover grew up to doghood, the pride and pet of the family, — and in truth a very handsome dog he was.

It is quite evident from his looks that his Newfoundland blood had been mingled with that of some other races; for he never attained the full size of that race, and his

points in some respects resembled those of a good setter.
He was grizzled black and white, and spotted on the sides
in litle inky drops about the size of a three-cent piece;
his hair was long and silky, his ears beautifully fringed,
and his tail long and feathery. His eyes were bright, soft,
and full of expression, and a jollier, livelier, more loving
creature never wore dog-skin. To be sure, his hunting
blood sometimes brought us and him into scrapes. A
neighbor now and then would call with a bill for ducks,
chickens, or young turkeys, which Rover had killed. The
last time this occurred it was decided that something must
be done; so Rover was shut up a whole day in a cold
lumber-room, with the murdered duck tied round his neck.
Poor fellow! how dejected and ashamed he looked, and

how grateful he was when his little friends would steal in to sit with him, and "poor" him in his disgrace! The punishment so improved his principles that he let poultry alone from that time, except now and then, when he would snap up a young chick or turkey, in pure absence of mind, before he really knew what he was about. We had great dread lest he should take to killing sheep, of which there were many flocks in the neighborhood. A dog which once kills sheep is a doomed beast, — as much as a man who has committed murder; and if our Rover, through the hunting blood that was in him, should once mistake a sheep for a deer, and kill him, we should be obliged to give him up to justice, — all his good looks and good qualities could not save him.

What anxieties his training under this head cost us! When we were driving out along the clean sandy roads, among the piny groves of Maine, it was half our enjoyment to see Rover, with ears and tail wild and flying with excitement and enjoyment, bounding and barking, now on this side the carriage, now on that, — now darting through the woods straight as an arrow, in his leaps after birds or squirrels, and anon returning to trot obediently by the carriage, and, wagging his tail, to ask applause for his performances. But anon a flock of sheep appeared in a distant field, and away would go Rover in full bow-wow, plunging in among them, scattering them hither and thither in dire confusion.

Then Johnny and Bill and all hands would spring from the
carriage in full chase of the rogue; and all of us shouted
vainly in the rear; and finally the rascal would be dragged
back, panting and crestfallen, to be admonished, scolded,
and cuffed with salutary discipline, heartily administered by
his best friends for the sake of saving his life. "Rover,
you naughty dog! Don't you know you must n't chase the
sheep? You 'll be killed, some of these days." Admoni-
tions of this kind, well shaken and thumped in, at last
seemed to reform him thoroughly. He grew so conscien-
tious, that, when a flock of sheep appeared on the side of
the road, he would immediately go to the other side of the
carriage, and turn away his head, rolling up his eyes
meanwhile to us for praise at his extraordinary good conduct. "Good dog, Rove! nice dog! good fellow! he does n't
touch the sheep, — no, he does n't." Such were the rewards
of virtue which sweetened his self-denial; hearing which,
he would plume up his feathery tail, and loll out his
tongue, with an air of virtuous assurance quite edifying to
behold.

Another of Rover's dangers was a habit he had of running races and cutting capers with the railroad engines as
they passed near our dwelling.

We lived in plain sight of the track, and three or four
times a day the old, puffing, smoky iron horse thundered
by, dragging his trains of cars, and making the very ground

shake under him. Rover never could resist the temptation
to run and bark, and race with so lively an antagonist;
and, to say the truth, John and Willy were somewhat of
his mind, — so that, though they were directed to catch
and hinder him, they entered so warmly into his own feelings that they never succeeded in breaking up the habit.
Every day when the distant whistle was heard, away would
go Rover, out of the door or through the window, — no
matter which, — race down to meet the cars, couch down
on the track in front of them, barking with all his might,
as if it were only a fellow-dog, and when they came so
near that escape seemed utterly impossible, he would lie
flat down between the rails and suffer the whole train to
pass over him, and then jump up and bark, full of glee, in
the rear. Sometimes he varied this performance more dangerously by jumping out full tilt between two middle cars
when the train had passed half-way over him. Everybody
predicted, of course, that he would be killed or maimed, and
the loss of a paw, or of his fine, saucy tail, was the least
of the dreadful things which were prophesied about him.
But Rover lived and throve in his imprudent courses notwithstanding.

The engineers and firemen, who began by throwing sticks
of wood and bits of coal at him, at last were quite subdued by his successful impudence, and came to consider
him as a regular institution of the railroad, and, if any

family excursion took him off for a day, they would inquire
with interest, "Where 's our dog? — what 's become of
Rover?" As to the female part of our family, we had
so often anticipated piteous scenes when poor Rover would
be brought home with broken paws or without his pretty
tail, that we quite used up our sensibilities, and concluded
that some kind angel, such as is appointed to watch over
little children's pets, must take special care of our Rover.

Rover had very tender domestic affections. His attachment to his little playfellows was most intense; and one
time, when all of them were taken off together on a week's
excursion, and Rover left alone at home, his low spirits
were really pitiful. He refused entirely to eat for the
first day, and finally could only be coaxed to take nour-
ishment, with many strokings and caresses, by being fed
out of Miss Anna's own hand. What perfectly boisterous
joy he showed when the children came back! — careering
round and round, picking up chips and bits of sticks, and
coming and offering them to one and another, in the ful-
ness of his doggish heart, to show how much he wanted
to give them something.

This mode of signifying his love by bringing something
in his mouth was one of his most characteristic tricks.
At one time he followed the carriage from Brunswick to
Bath, and in the streets of the city somehow lost his
way, so that he was gone all night. Many a little heart

went to bed anxious and sorrowful for the loss of its shaggy playfellow that night, and Rover doubtless was remembered in many little prayers ; what, therefore, was the joy of being awakened by a joyful barking under the window the next morning, when his little friends rushed in their nightgowns to behold Rover back again, fresh and frisky, bearing in his mouth a branch of a tree about six feet long, as his offering of joy.

When the family removed to Zion Hill, Rover went with them, the trusty and established family friend. Age had somewhat matured his early friskiness. Perhaps the grave neighborhood of a theological seminary and the responsibility of being a Professor's dog might have something to do with it, but Rover gained an established character as a dog of respectable habits, and used to march to the post-office at the heels of his master twice a day, as regularly as any theological student.

Little Charley the second — the youngest of the brood, who took the place of our lost little Prince Charley — was yet padding about in short robes, and seemed to regard Rover in the light of a discreet older brother, and Rover's manners to him were of most protecting gentleness. Charley seemed to consider Rover in all things as such a model, that he overlooked the difference between a dog and a boy, and wearied himself with fruitless attempts to scratch his ear with his foot as Rover did, and one day was brought in dripping from a neighboring swamp, where he had been lying down in the water, because Rover did.

Once in a while a wild oat or two from Rover's old sack would seem to entangle him. Sometimes, when we were driving out, he would, in his races after the carriage, make a flying leap into a farmer's yard, and, if he lighted in a flock of chickens or turkeys, gobble one off-hand, and be off again and a mile ahead before the mother hen had recovered from her astonishment. Sometimes, too, he would have a race with the steam-engine just for old acquaintance' sake. But these were comparatively transient follies; in general, no members of the grave institutions around him behaved with more dignity and decorum than Rover. He tried to listen to his master's theological lectures, and to attend chapel on Sundays; but the prejudices of society were against him, and so he meekly submitted to be shut out, and waited outside the door on these occasions.

He formed a part of every domestic scene. At family prayers, stretched out beside his master, he looked up reflectively with his great soft eyes, and seemed to join in the serious feeling of the hour. When all were gay, when singing, or frolicking, or games were going on, Rover barked and frisked in higher glee than any. At night it was his joy to stretch his furry length by our bedside, where he slept with one ear on cock for any noise which it might be his business to watch and attend to. It was comfort to hear the tinkle of his collar when he moved in the night, or to be wakened by his cold nose pushed against one's hand if one slept late in the morning. And then he was always so glad when we woke; and when any member of the family circle was gone for a few days, Rover's warm delight and welcome were not the least of the pleasures of return.

And what became of him? Alas! the fashion came up of poisoning dogs, and this poor, good, fond, faithful creature was enticed into swallowing poisoned meat. One day he came in suddenly, ill and frightened, and ran to the friends who always had protected him, — but in vain. In a few moments he was in convulsions, and all the tears and sobs of his playfellows could not help him; he closed his bright, loving eyes, and died in their arms.

If those who throw poison to dogs could only see the real grief it brings into a family to lose the friend and playfellow who has grown up with the children, and shared their plays, and been for years in every family scene, — if they could know how sorrowful it is to see the poor dumb friend suffer agonies which they cannot relieve, — if they could see all this, we have faith to believe they never would do so more.

Our poor Rover was buried with decent care near the house, and a mound of petunias over him kept his memory ever bright; but it will be long before his friends will get another as true.

III.

AFTER the sad fate of Rover, there came a long in- terval in which we had no dog. Our hearts were too sore to want another. His collar, tied with black crape, hung under a pretty engraving of Landseer's, called "My Dog," which we used to fancy to be an exact resemblance of our pet.

The children were some of them grown up and gone to school, or scattered about the world. If ever the question of another dog was agitated, papa cut it short with, "I won't have another; I won't be made to feel again as I did about Rover." But somehow Mr. Charley the younger got his eye on a promising litter of puppies, and at last he begged papa into consenting that he might have one of them.

It was a little black mongrel, of no particular race or breed, — a mere common cur, without any pretensions to family, but the best-natured, jolliest little low-bred pup that ever boy had for a playmate. To be sure, he had the usual puppy sins; he would run away with papa's slippers. and boots, and stockings; he would be under everybody's feet, at the most inconvenient moment; he chewed up a hearth-broom or two, and pulled one of Charley's caps to pieces in the night, with an industry worthy of a better

cause ; — still, because he was dear to Charley, papa and
mamma winked very hard at his transgressions.

The name of this little black individual was Stromion,
— a name taken from a German fairy tale, which the Professor was very fond of reading in the domestic circle ; and
Stromion, by dint of much patience, much feeding, and very
indulgent treatment, grew up into a very fat, common-look-
ing black cur dog, not very prepossessing in appearance
and manners, but possessed of the very best heart in the
world, and most inconceivably affectionate and good-natured.
Sometimes some of the older members of the family would
trouble Charley's enjoyment in his playfellow by suggesting
that he was no blood dog, and that he belonged to no particular dog family that could be named.   Papa comforted
him by the assurance that Stromion did belong to a very
old and respectable breed, — that he was a *mongrel ;* and
Charley after that valued him excessively under this head ;
and if any one tauntingly remarked that Stromion was
only a cur, he would flame up in his defence, — " He is n't
a cur, he 's a mongrel," introducing him to strangers with
the addition to all his other virtues, that he was a " pure
mongrel, — papa says so."

The edict against dogs in the family having once been
broken down, Master Will proceeded to gratify his own
impulses, and soon led home to the family circle an enor-
mous old black Newfoundland, of pure breed, which had

been presented him by a man who was leaving the place. Prince was in the decline of his days, but a fine, majestic old fellow. He had a sagacity and capacity of personal affection which were uncommon. Many dogs will change from master to master without the least discomposure. A good bone will compensate for any loss of the heart, and make a new friend seem quite as good as an old one. But Prince had his affections quite as distinctly as a human being, and we learned this to our sorrow when he had to be weaned from his old master under our roof. His howls and lamentations were so dismal and protracted, that the house could not contain him ; we were obliged to put him into an outhouse to compose his mind, and we still have a vivid image of him sitting, the picture of despair, over an untasted mutton shank, with his nose in the air, and the most dismal howls proceeding from his mouth. Time, the comforter, however, assuaged his grief, and he came at last to transfer all his stores of affection to Will, and to consider himself once more as a dog with a master.

Prince used to inhabit his young master's apartment, from the window of which he would howl dismally when Will left him to go to the academy near by, and yelp triumphant welcomes when he saw him returning. He was really and passionately fond of music, and, though strictly forbidden the parlor, would push and elbow his way there with dogged determination when there was playing or singing.

Any one who should have seen Prince's air when he had a point to carry, would understand why quiet obstinacy is called doggedness.

The female members of the family, seeing that two dogs had gained admission to the circle, had cast their eyes admiringly on a charming little Italian greyhound, that was living in doleful captivity at a dog-fancier's in Boston, and resolved to set him free and have him for their own. Accordingly they returned one day in triumph, with him in their arms, — a fair, delicate creature, white as snow, except one mouse-colored ear. He was received with enthusiasm, and christened Giglio; the honors of his first bath and toilette were performed by Mademoiselles the young ladies on their knees, as if he had been in reality young Prince Giglio from fairy-land.

Of all beautiful shapes in dog form, never was there one more perfect than this. His hair shone like spun glass, and his skin was as fine and pink as that of a baby; his paws and ears were translucent like fine china, and he had great, soft, tremulous dark eyes; his every movement seemed more graceful than the last. Whether running or leaping, or sitting in graceful attitudes on the parlor table among the ladies' embroidery-frames, with a great rose-colored bow under his throat, he was alike a thing of beauty, and his beauty alone won all hearts to him.

When the papa first learned that a third dog had been

introduced into the household, his patience gave way. The thing was getting desperate; we were being overrun with dogs; our house was no more a house, but a kennel; it ought to be called Cunopolis,—a city of dogs; he could not and would not have it so; but papa, like most other indulgent old gentlemen, was soon reconciled to the children's pets. In fact, Giglio was found cowering under the bed-clothes at the Professor's feet not two mornings after his arrival, and the good gentleman descended with him in his arms to breakfast, talking to him in the most devoted manner:—"Poor little Giglio, was he cold last night? and

8

did he want to get into papa's bed? he should be brought
down stairs, that he should"; — all which, addressed to a
young rascal whose sinews were all like steel, and who
could have jumped from the top stair to the bottom like a
feather, was sufficiently amusing.

Giglio's singular beauty and grace were his only merits;
he had no love nor power of loving; he liked to be petted
and kept warm, but it mattered nothing to him who did it.
He was as ready to run off with a stranger as with his
very best friend, — would follow any whistle or any caller,
— was, in fact, such a gay rover, that we came very near
losing him many times; and more than once he was brought
back from the Boston cars, on board which he had followed
a stranger.   He also had, we grieve to say, very careless
habits; and after being washed white as snow, and adorned
with choice rose-colored ribbons, would be brought back
soiled and ill-smelling from a neighbor's livery-stable, where
he had been indulging in low society.   For all that, he was
very lordly and aristocratic in his airs with poor Stromion,
who was a dog with a good, loving heart, if he was black
and homely.   Stromion admired Giglio with the most evident
devotion; he would always get up to give him the warm
corner, and would sit humbly in the distance and gaze on
him with most longing admiration, — for all of which my
fine gentleman rewarded him only with an occasional snarl
or a nip, as he went by him.   Sometimes Giglio would con-

descend to have a romp with Stromion for the sake of passing the time, and then Stromion would be perfectly delighted, and frisk and roll his clumsy body over the carpet with his graceful antagonist, all whose motions were a study for an artist. When Giglio was tired of play, he would give Stromion a nip that would send him yelping from the field; and then he would tick, tick gracefully away to some embroidered ottoman forbidden to all but himself, where he would sit graceful and classical as some Etruscan vase, and look down superior on the humble companion who looked up to him with respectful admiration.

Giglio knew his own good points, and was possessed with the very spirit of a coquette. He would sometimes obstinately refuse the caresses and offered lap of his mistresses, and seek to ingratiate himself with some stolid theological visitor, for no other earthly purpose that we could see than that he was determined to make himself the object of attention. We have seen him persist in jumping time and again on the hard, bony knees of some man who hated dogs, and did not mean to notice him, until he won attention and caresses, when immediately he would spring down and tick away perfectly contented. He assumed lofty, fine-gentleman airs with Prince also, for which sometimes he got his reward,—for Prince, the old, remembered that he was a dog of blood, and would not take any nonsense from him.

Like many old dogs, Prince had a very powerful doggy smell, which was a great personal objection to him, and Giglio was always in a civil way making reflections upon this weak point. Prince was fond of indulging himself with an afternoon nap on the door-mat, and sometimes when he rose from his repose, Giglio would spring gracefully from the table where he had been overlooking him, and, picking his way daintily to the mat, would snuff at it, with his long, thin nose, with an air of extreme disgust. It was evidently a dog insult, done according to the politest modes of refined society, and said as plain as words could say, — "My dear sir, excuse me, but can you tell what makes this peculiar smell where you have been lying?" At any rate, Prince understood the sarcasm, for a deep angry growl and a sharp nip would now and then teach my fine gentleman to mind his own business.

Giglio's lot at last was to travel in foreign lands, for his young mistresses, being sent to school in Paris, took him with them to finish his education and acquire foreign graces. He was smuggled on board the Fulton, and placed in an upper berth, well wrapped in a blanket; and the last we saw of him was his long, thin Italian nose, and dark, tremulous eyes looking wistfully at us from the folds of the flannel in which he shivered. Sensitiveness to cold was one of his great peculiarities. In winter he wore little blankets, which his fond mistresses made with anxious

care, and on which his initials were embroidered with
their own hands. In the winter weather on Zion Hill he
was often severely put to it to gratify his love of roving in
the cold snows ; he would hold up first one leg, and then
the other, and contrive to get along on three, so as to save
himself as much as possible ; and more than once he caught
severe colds, requiring careful nursing and medical treatment to bring him round again.

The Fulton sailed early in March. It was chilly, stormy
weather, so that the passengers all suffered somewhat with
cold, and Master Giglio was glad to lie rolled in his blanket, looking like a sea-sick gentleman. The captain very
generously allowed him a free passage, and in pleasant
weather he used to promenade the deck, where his beauty
won for him caresses and attentions innumerable. The stew-
ards and cooks always had choice morsels for him, and fed
him to such a degree as would have spoiled any other
dog's figure ; but his could not be spoiled. All the ladies
vied with each other in seeking his good graces, and after
dinner he pattered from one to another, to be fed with
sweet things and confectionery, and hear his own praises,
like a gay buck of fashion as he was.

Landed in Paris, he met a warm reception at the Pen-
sion of Madame B——; but ambition filled his breast. He
was in the great, gay city of Paris, the place where a
handsome dog has but to appear to make his fortune, and

so Giglio resolved to seek out for himself a more brilliant destiny.

One day, when he was being led to take the air in the court, he slipped his leash, sped through the gate, and away down the street like the wind. It was idle to attempt to follow him; he was gone like a bird in the air, and left the hearts of his young mistresses quite desolate.

Some months after, as they were one evening eating ices in the Champs Elysées, a splendid carriage drove up, from which descended a liveried servant, with a dog in his arms. It was Giglio, the faithless Giglio, with his one mouse-colored ear, that marked him from all other dogs! He had evidently accomplished his destiny, and become the darling of rank and fashion, rode in an elegant carriage, and had a servant in livery devoted to him. Of course he did not pretend to notice his former friends. The footman, who had come out apparently to give him an airing, led him up and down close by where they were sitting, and bestowed on him the most devoted attentions. Of course there was no use in trying to reclaim him, and so they took their last look of the fair inconstant, and left him to his brilliant destiny. And thus ends the history of PRINCE GIGLIO.

IV.

AFTER Prince Giglio deserted us and proved so faithless, we were for a while determined not to have
another pet.   They were all good for nothing, — all alike
ungrateful ; we forswore the whole race of dogs.   But the
next winter we went to live in the beautiful city of Florence, in Italy, and there, in spite of all our protestations,
our hearts were again ensnared.

You must know that in the neighborhood of Florence
is a celebrated villa, owned by a Russian nobleman, Prince
Demidoff, and that among other fine things that are to
be found there are a very nice breed of King Charles
spaniels, which are called Demidoffs, after the place.   One
of these, a pretty little creature, was presented to us by a
kind lady, and our resolution against having any more pets
all melted away in view of the soft, beseeching eyes, the
fine, silky ears, the glossy, wavy hair, and bright chestnut paws of the new favorite.   She was exactly such a
pretty creature as one sees painted in some of the splendid old Italian pictures, and which Mr. Ruskin describes as
belonging to the race of "fringy paws."   The little creature
was warmly received among us ; an ottoman was set apart
for her to lie on ; and a bright bow of green, red, and
white ribbon, the Italian colors, was prepared for her neck ;
and she was christened Florence, after her native city.

Florence was a perfect little fine lady, and a perfect Italian, — sensitive, intelligent, nervous, passionate, and constant in her attachments, but with a hundred little whims and fancies that required petting and tending hourly. She was perfectly miserable if she was not allowed to attend us in our daily drives, yet in the carriage she was so excitable and restless, so interested to take part in everything she saw and heard in the street, that it was all we could do to hold her in and make her behave herself decently. She was nothing but a little bundle of nerves, apparently all the while in a tremble of excitement about one thing or another ; she was so disconsolate if left at home, that she went everywhere with us. She visited the picture-galleries, the museums, and all the approved sights of Florence, and improved her mind as much as many other young ladies who do the same.

Then we removed from Florence to Rome, and poor Flo was direfully sea-sick on board the steamboat, in company with all her young mistresses, but recovered herself at Civita Vecchia, and entered Rome in high feather. There she settled herself complacently in our new lodgings, which were far more spacious and elegant than those we had left in Florence, and began to claim her little rights in all the sight-seeing of the Eternal City.

She went with us to palaces and to ruins, scrambling up and down, hither and thither, with the utmost show of interest. She went up all the stairs to the top of the Capitol, except the very highest and last, where she put on airs, whimpered, and professed such little frights, that her mistress was forced to carry her; but once on top, she barked from right to left, — now at the snowy top of old Soracte, now at the great, wide, desolate plains of the Campagna, and now at the old ruins of the Roman Forum down under our feet. Upon all she had her own opinion, and was not backward to express herself. At other times she used to ride with us to a beautiful country villa out-

side of the walls of Rome, called the Pamfili Doria. How
beautiful and lovely this place was I can scarcely tell my
little friends. There were long alleys and walks of the
most beautiful trees ; there were winding paths leading to
all manner of beautiful grottos, and charming fountains,
and the wide lawns used to be covered with the most
lovely flowers. There were anemones that looked like little
tulips, growing about an inch and a half high, and of all
colors, — blue, purple, lilac, pink, crimson, and white, — and
there were great beds of fragrant blue and white violets.
As to the charming grace and beauty of the fountains that
were to be found here and there all through the grounds,
I could not describe them to you. They were made of
marble, carved in all sorts of fanciful devices, and grown
over with green mosses and maidenhair.

What spirits little Miss Flo had, when once set down in
these enchanting fields! While all her mistresses were
gathering lapfuls of many-colored anemones, violets, and all
sorts of beautiful things, Flo would snuff the air, and run
and race hither and thither, with her silky ears flying and
her whole little body quivering with excitement. Now she
would race round the grand basin of a fountain, and bark
with all her might at the great white swans that were
swelling and ruffling their silver-white plumage, and took
her noisy attentions with all possible composure. Then she
would run off down some long side-alley after a lot of

French soldiers, whose gay red legs and blue coats seemed
to please her mightily; and many a fine chase she gave
her mistresses, who were obliged to run up and down, here,
there, and everywhere, to find her when they wanted to go
home again.

One time my lady's friskiness brought her into quite a
serious trouble, as you shall hear. We were all going to
St. Peter's Church, and just as we came to the bridge of
St. Angelo, that crosses the Tiber, we met quite a con-
course of carriages. Up jumped my lady Florence, all alive
and busy, — for she always reckoned everything that was
going on a part of her business, — and gave such a spring
that over she went, sheer out of the carriage, into the
mixed medley of carriages, horses, and people below. We
were all frightened enough, but not half so frightened as
she was, as she ran blindly down a street, followed by a
perfect train of ragged little black-eyed, black-haired boys,
all shouting and screaming after her. As soon as he could,
our courier got down and ran after her, but he might as
well have chased a streak of summer lightning. She was
down the street, round the corner, and lost to view, with
all the ragamuffin tribe, men, boys, and women, after her;
and so we thought we had lost her, and came home to our
lodgings very desolate in heart, when lo! our old porter
told us that a little dog that looked like ours had come
begging and whining at our street door, but before he could

open it the poor little wanderer had been chased away
again and gone down the street. After a while some very
polite French soldiers picked her up in the Piazza di Spagna,
— a great public square near our dwelling, to get into which
we were obliged to go down some one or two hundred
steps. We could fancy our poor Flo, frightened and panting, flying like a meteor down these steps, till she was
brought up by the arms of a soldier below.

Glad enough were we when the polite soldier brought
her back to our doors;—and one must say one good thing
for French soldiers all the world over, that they are the
pleasantest-tempered and politest people possible, so very
tender-hearted towards all sorts of little defenceless pets, so
that our poor runaway could not have fallen into better
hands.

After this, we were careful to hold her more firmly when
she had her little nervous starts and struggles in riding
about Rome.

One day we had been riding outside of the walls of the
city, and just as we were returning home we saw coming
towards us quite a number of splendid carriages with
prancing black horses. It was the Pope and several of
his cardinals coming out for an afternoon airing. The carriages stopped, and the Pope and cardinals all got out to
take a little exercise on foot, and immediately all carriages
that were in the way drew to one side, and those of the

people in them who were Roman Catholics got out and knelt down to wait for the Pope's blessing as he went by. As for us, we were contented to wait sitting in the carriage.

On came the Pope, looking like a fat, mild, kind-hearted old gentleman, smiling and blessing the people as he went on, and the cardinals scuffing along in the dust behind him. He walked very near to our carriage, and Miss Florence, notwithstanding all our attempts to keep her decent, would give a smart little bow-wow right in his face just as he was passing. He smiled benignly, and put out his hand in sign of blessing toward our carriage, and Florence doubtless got what she had been asking for.

From Rome we travelled to Naples, and Miss Flo went with us through our various adventures there, — up Mount Vesuvius, where she half choked herself with sulphurous smoke. There is a place near Naples called the Solfatara, which is thought to be the crater of the extinct volcano, where there is a cave that hisses, and roars, and puffs out scalding steam like a perpetual locomotive, and all the ground around shakes and quivers as if it were only a crust over some terrible abyss. The pools of water are all white with sulphur; the ground is made of sulphur and arsenic and all such sort of uncanny matters; and we were in a fine fright lest Miss Florence, being in one of her wildest and most indiscreet moods, should tumble into some burning hole, or strangle herself with sulphur; and in fact she rolled over and over in a sulphur puddle, and then, scampering off, rolled in ashes by way of cleaning herself. We could not, however, leave her at home during any of our excursions, and so had to make the best of these imprudences.

When at last the time came for us to leave Italy, we were warned that Florence would not be allowed to travel in the railroad cars in the French territories. All dogs, of all sizes and kinds, whose owners wish to have travel with them, are shut up in a sort of closet by themselves, called the dog-car; and we thought our nervous, excitable little pet would be frightened into fits, to be separated from all her friends, and made to travel with all sorts of strange dogs. So we determined to smuggle her along in a basket. At Turin we bought a little black basket, just big enough to contain her, and into it we made her go, — very sorely against her will, as we could not explain to her the reason why. Very guilty indeed we felt, with this travelling conveyance hung on one arm, sitting in the waiting-room, and dreading every minute lest somebody should see the great bright eyes peeping through the holes of the basket, or hear the subdued little whines and howls which every now and then came from its depths.

Florence had been a petted lady, used to having her own way, and a great deal of it; and this being put up in a little black basket, where she could neither make her remarks on the scenery, nor join in the conversation of her young mistresses, seemed to her a piece of caprice without rhyme or reason. So every once in a while she would express her mind on the subject by a sudden dismal little whine; and what was specially trying, she would take the occasion to do this when the cars stopped and all was quiet, so that everybody could hear her. Where's that dog? — somebody's got a dog in here, — was the inquiry very plain to be seen in the suspicious looks which the guard cast upon us as he put his head into our compartment, and gazed about inquiringly. Finally, to our great terror, a railway director, a tall, gentlemanly man, took his seat in our very compartment, where Miss Florence's basket garnished the pocket above our heads, and she was in one of her most querulous moods. At every stopping-place she gave her little sniffs and howls, and rattled her basket so as to draw all eyes. We all tried to look innocent and unconscious, but the polite railroad director very easily perceived what was the matter. He looked from one anxious, half-laughing face to the others, with a kindly twinkle in his eye, but said nothing. All the guards and *employés* bowed down to him, and came cap in hand at every stopping-place to take his orders. What a relief it was to hear him say, in a low voice, to them: "These young ladies have a little dog which they are carrying. Take no notice of it, and do not disturb them!" Of

course, after that, though Florence barked and howled and
rattled her basket, and sometimes showed her great eyes,
like two coal-black diamonds, through its lattice-work,
nobody saw and nobody heard, and we came unmolested
with her to Paris.

After a while she grew accustomed to her little travelling carriage, and resigned herself quietly to go to sleep
in it; and so we got her from Paris to Kent, where we
stopped a few days to visit some friends in a lovely country place called Swaylands.

Here we had presented to us another pet, that was
ever after the chosen companion and fast friend of Florence. He was a little Skye terrier, of the color of a Mal-
tese cat, covered all over with fine, long, silky hair, which
hung down so evenly, that it was difficult at the first glance
to say which was his head and which his tail. But at the
head end there gleamed out a pair of great, soft, speaking
eyes, that formed the only beauty of the creature; and
very beautiful they were, in their soft, beseeching loving-
ness.

Poor Rag had the tenderest heart that ever was hid in
a bundle of hair; he was fidelity and devotion itself, and
used to lie at our feet in the railroad carriages as still as
a gray sheep-skin, only too happy to be there on any
terms. It would be too long to tell our travelling adventures in England; suffice it to say, that at last we went

on board the Africa to come home, with our two pets, which had to be handed over to the butcher, and slept on quarters of mutton and sides of beef, till they smelt of tallow and grew fat in a most vulgar way.

At last both of them were safely installed in the brown stone cottage in Andover, and Rag was presented to a young lady to whom he had been sent as a gift from England, and to whom he attached himself with the most faithful devotion.

Both dogs insisted on having their part of the daily walks and drives of their young mistresses; and, when they observed them putting on their hats, would run, and bark, and leap, and make as much noise as a family of children clamoring for a ride.

After a few months, Florence had three or four little puppies. Very puny little things they were; and a fierce, nervous little mother she made. Her eyes looked blue as burnished steel, and if anybody only set foot in the room where her basket was, her hair would bristle, and she would bark so fiercely as to be quite alarming. For all that, her little ones proved quite a failure, for they were all stone-blind. In vain we waited and hoped and watched for nine days, and long after; the eyes were glazed and dim, and one by one they died. The last two seemed to promise to survive, and were familiarly known in the family circle by the names of Milton and Beethoven.

9

But the fatigues of nursing exhausted the delicate constitution of poor Florence, and she lay all one day in spasms.
It became evident that a tranquil passage must be secured
for Milton and Beethoven to the land of shades, or their
little mother would go there herself; and accordingly they
vanished from this life.

As to poor Flo, the young medical student in the family
took her into a water-cure course of treatment, wrapping
her in a wet napkin first, and then in his scarlet flannel
dressing-gown, and keeping a wet cloth with iced water
round her head. She looked out of her wrappings, patient
and pitiful, like a very small old African female, in a very
serious state of mind. To the glory of the water-cure,
however, this course in one day so cured her, that she
was frisking about the next, happy as if nothing had happened.

She had, however, a slight attack of the spasms, which
caused her to run frantically and cry to have the hall-door
opened ; and when it was opened, she scampered up in all
haste into the chamber of her medical friend, and, not
finding him there, jumped upon his bed, and began with
her teeth and paws to get around her the scarlet dressing-
gown in which she had found relief before. So she was
again packed in wet napkins, and after that never had
another attack.

After this, Florence was begged from us by a lady who

fell in love with her beautiful eyes, and she went to reside
in a most lovely cottage in H——, where she received
the devoted attentions of a whole family. The family
physician, however, fell violently in love with her, and, by
dint of caring for her in certain little ailments, awakened
such a sentiment in return, that at last she was given to
him, and used to ride about in state with him in his carriage, visiting his patients, and giving her opinion on their
symptoms.

At last her health grew delicate and her appetite failed.
In vain chicken, and chops, and all the delicacies that could
tempt the most fastidious, were offered to her, cooked ex-
pressly for her table; the end of all things fair must come,
and poor Florence breathed her last, and was put into a
little rosewood casket, lined with white, and studded with
silver nails, and so buried under a fine group of chestnuts
in the grounds of her former friends. A marble tablet was
to be affixed to one of these, commemorating her charms;
but, like other spoiled beauties, her memory soon faded,
and the tablet has been forgotten.

The mistress of Rag, who is devoted to his memory, insists that not enough space has been given in this memoir
to his virtues. But the virtues of honest Rag were of that
kind which can be told in a few sentences, — a warm, loving heart, a boundless desire to be loved, and a devotion
that made him regard with superstitious veneration all the

movements of his mistress. The only shrewd trick he possessed was a habit of drawing on her sympathy by feigning
a lame leg whenever she scolded or corrected him. In his
English days he had had an injury from the kick of a
horse, which, however, had long since been healed; but he
remembered the petting he got for this infirmity, and so
recalled it whenever he found that his mistress's stock of
affection was running low. A blow or a harsh word would
cause him to limp in an alarming manner; but a few
caresses would set matters all straight again.

Rag had been a frantic ratter, and often roused the
whole family by his savage yells after rats that he heard
gambolling quite out of his reach behind the partitions in
the china closet. He would crouch his head on his fore-
paws, and lie watching at rat-holes, in hopes of intercepting
some transient loafer; and one day he actually broke the
back and bones of a gray old thief whom he caught ma-
rauding in the china closet.

Proud and happy was he of this feat; but, poor fellow!
he had to repose on the laurels thus gained, for his teeth
were old and poor, and more than one old rebel slipped
away from him, leaving him screaming with disappointed
ambition.

At last poor Rag became aged and toothless, and a
shake which he one day received from a big dog, who took
him for a bundle of wick-yarn, hastened the breaking up

of his constitution.   He was attacked with acute rheumatism, and, notwithstanding the most assiduous cares of his
mistress, died at last in her arms.

Funeral honors were decreed him ; white chrysanthemums
and myrtle leaves decked his bier.   And so Rag was gathered to the dogs which had gone before him.

V.

WELL, after the departure of Madam Florence there
was a long cessation of the dog mania in our family.   We concluded that we would have no more pets ; for
they made too much anxiety, and care, and trouble, and
broke all our hearts by death or desertion.

At last, however, some neighbors of ours took unto themselves, to enliven their dwelling, a little saucy Scotch terrier, whose bright eyes and wicked tricks so wrought upon
the heart of one of our juvenile branches, that there was
no rest in the camp without this addition to it.   Nothing
was so pretty, so bright, so knowing and cunning, as a
" Scotch terrier," and a Scotch terrier we must have, — so
said Miss Jenny, our youngest.

And so a bargain was struck by one of Jenny's friends
with some of the knowing ones in Boston, and home she
came, the happy possessor of a genuine article, — as wide

awake, impertinent, frisky, and wicked a little elf as ever
was covered with a shock of rough tan-colored hair.

His mistress no sooner gazed on him, than she was inspired to give him a name suited to his peculiar character;
— so he frisked into the front door announced as Wix, and
soon made himself perfectly at home in the family circle,
which he took, after his own fashion, by storm. He entered
the house like a small whirlwind, dashed, the first thing,
into the Professor's study, seized a slipper which was dang-
ling rather uncertainly on one of his studious feet, and,
wresting it off, raced triumphantly with it around the hall,
barking distractedly every minute that he was not shaking
and worrying his prize.

Great was the sensation. Grandma tottered with trembling steps to the door, and asked, with hesitating tones,
what sort of a creature that might be ; and being saluted
with the jubilant proclamation, "Why, Grandma, it's my
dog, — a real genuine, Scotch terrier ; he'll never grow any
larger, and he's a perfect beauty ! don't you think so?" —
Grandma could only tremblingly reply, "O, there is not
any danger of his going mad, is there? Is he generally so
playful?"

Playful was certainly a mild term for the tempest of excitement in which master Wix flew round and round in
giddy circles, springing over ottomans, diving under sofas,
barking from beneath chairs, and resisting every effort to

recapture the slipper with bristling hair and blazing eyes, as if the whole of his dog-life consisted in keeping his prize; till at length he caught a glimpse of pussy's tail, — at which, dropping the slipper, he precipitated himself after the flying meteor, tumbling, rolling, and scratching down the kitchen stairs, and standing on his hind-legs barking distractedly at poor Tom, who had taken refuge in the sink, and sat with his tail magnified to the size of a small bolster.

This cat, the most reputable and steady individual of his species, the darling of the most respectable of cooks, had received the name of Thomas Henry, by which somewhat lengthy appellation he was generally designated in the family circle, as a mark of the respect which his serious and contemplative manner commonly excited. Thomas had but one trick of popularity. With much painstaking and care the cook had taught him the act of performing a somerset over our hands when held at a decent height from the floor; and for this one elegant accomplishment, added to great success in his calling of rat-catching, he was held in great consideration in the family, and had meandered his decorous way about house, slept in the sun, and otherwise conducted himself with the innocent and tranquil freedom which became a family cat of correct habits and a good conscience.

The irruption of Wix into our establishment was like

the bursting of a bomb at the feet of some respectable citizen going tranquilly to market. Thomas was a cat of courage, and rats of the largest size shrunk appalled at the very sight of his whiskers ; but now he sat in the sink quite cowed, consulting with great, anxious yellow eyes the throng of faces that followed Wix down the stairs, and watching anxiously the efforts Miss Jenny was making to subdue and quiet him.

"Wix, you naughty little rascal, you must n't bark at Thomas Henry; be still !" Whereat Wix, understanding himself to be blamed, brought forth his trump card of accomplishments, which he always offered by way of pacification whenever he was scolded. He reared himself up on his hind-legs, hung his head languishingly on one side, lolled out his tongue, and made a series of supplicatory gestures with his fore-paws, — a trick which never failed to bring down the house in a storm of applause, and carry him out of any scrape with flying colors.

Poor Thomas Henry, from his desolate sink, saw his terrible rival carried off in Miss Jenny's arms amid the applauses of the whole circle, and had abundance of time to reflect on the unsubstantial nature of popularity. After that he grew dejected and misanthropic, — a real Cardinal Wolsey in furs, — for Wix was possessed with a perfect cat-hunting mania, and, whenever he was not employed in other mischief, was always ready for a bout with Thomas Henry.

It is true, he sometimes came back from these encounters with a scratched and bloody nose, for Thomas Henry was a cat of no mean claw, and would turn to bay at times; but generally he felt the exertion too much for his advanced years and quiet habits, and so for safety he passed much of his time in the sink, over the battlements of which he would leisurely survey the efforts of the enemy to get at him. The cook hinted strongly of the danger of rheumatism to her favorite from these damp quarters, but Wix at present was the reigning favorite, and it was vain to dispute his sway.

Next to Thomas Henry, Wix directed his principal efforts to teasing Grandmamma. Something or other about her black dress and quiet movements seemed to suggest to him suspicions. He viewed her as something to be narrowly watched; he would lie down under some chair or table, and watch her motions with his head on his fore-paws as if he were watching at a rat-hole. She evidently was not a rat, he seemed to say to himself, but who knows what she may be; and he would wink at her with his great bright eyes, and, if she began to get up, would spring from his ambush and bark at her feet with frantic energy, — by which means he nearly threw her over two or three times.

His young mistress kept a rod, and put him through a severe course of discipline for these offences; after which

he grew more careful, — but still the unaccountable fascina-
tion seemed to continue ; still he would lie in ambush, and,
though forbidden to bark, would dart stealthily forward
when he saw her preparing to rise, and be under her dress
smelling in a suspicious manner at her heels. He would
spring from his place at the fire, and rush to the staircase
when he heard her leisurely step descending the stairs,
and once or twice nearly overset her by being under her
heels, bringing on himself a chastisement which he in
vain sought to avert by the most vigorous deprecatory
pawing.

Grandmamma's favorite evening employment was to sit
sleeping in her chair, gradually bobbing her head lower
and lower, — all which movements Wix would watch, giving
a short snap, or a suppressed growl, at every bow. What
he would have done, if, as John Bunyan says, he had been
allowed to have his "doggish way" with her, it is impossible to say. Once he succeeded in seizing the slipper
from her foot as she sat napping, and a glorious race he
had with it, — out at the front door, up the path to the
Theological Seminary, and round and round the halls con-
secrated to better things, with all the glee of an imp. At
another time he made a dart into her apartment, and
seized a turkey-wing which the good old lady had used
for a duster, and made such a regular forenoon's work of
worrying, shaking, and teasing it, that every feather in it
was utterly demolished.

In fact, there was about Wix something so elfish and unpish, that there began to be shrewd suspicions that he must be somehow or other a descendant of the celebrated poodle of Faust, and that one need not be surprised some day to have him suddenly looming up into some uncanny shape, or entering into conversation, and uttering all sorts of improprieties unbefitting a theological professor's family.

He had a persistence in wicked ways that resisted the most energetic nurture and admonition of his young mistress. His combativeness was such, that a peaceable walk down the fashionable street of Zion Hill in his company became impossible ; all was race and scurry, cackle and flutter, wherever he appeared, — hens and poultry flying, frightened cats mounting trees with magnified tails, dogs yelping and snarling, and children and cows running in every direction. No modest young lady could possibly walk out in company with such a son of confusion. Beside this, Wix had his own private inexplicable personal piques against different visitors in the family, and in the most unexpected moment would give a snap or a nip to the most unoffending person. His friends in the family circle dropped off. His ways were pronounced too bad, his conduct perfectly indefensible ; his young mistress alone clung to him, and declared that her vigorous system of education would at last reform his eccentricities, and turn him out a tip-top dog. But when he would slyly leave home, and, after rolling and steeping himself in the ill-smelling deposits of the stable or drain, come home and spring with impudent ease into her lap, or put himself to sleep on her little white bed, the magic cords of affection gave out, and disgust began to succeed. It began to be remarked that this was a stable-dog, educated for the coach-boy and stable, and to be doubted whether it was worth while to endeavor to raise him to a lady's boudoir; and so at last, when the family removed from Zion Hill, he was taken back and disposed of at a somewhat reduced price.

Since then, as we are informed, he has risen to fame and honor. His name has even appeared in sporting gazettes as the most celebrated "ratter" in little Boston, and his mistress was solemnly assured by his present possessor that for "cat work" he was unequalled, and that he would not take fifty dollars for him. From all which it appears that a dog which is only a torment and a nuisance in one sphere may be an eminent character in another.

The catalogue of our dogs ends with Wix. Whether we shall ever have another or not we cannot tell, but in the following pages I will tell my young readers a few true stories of other domestic pets which may amuse them.

DOGS AND CATS

A ND now, with all and each of the young friends who have read these little histories of our dogs, we want to have a few moments of quiet chat about dogs and household pets in general.

In these stories you must have noticed that each dog had as much his own character as if he had been a human being. Carlo was not like Rover, nor Rover like Giglio, nor Giglio like Florence, nor Florence like Rag, nor Rag like Wix,—any more than Charley is like Fred, or Fred

like Henry, or Henry like Eliza, or Eliza like Julia. Every
animal has his own character, as marked and distinct as a
human being. Many people who have not studied much
into the habits of animals don't know this. To them a
dog is a dog, a cat a cat, a horse a horse, and no more,—
that is the end of it.

But domestic animals that associate with human beings
develop a very different character from what they would
possess in a wild state. Dogs, for example, in those countries where there is a prejudice against receiving them
into man's association, herd together, and become wild and
fierce like wolves. This is the case in many Oriental
countries, where there are superstitious ideas about dogs;
as, for instance, that they are unclean and impure. But in
other countries, the dog, for the most part, forsakes all
other dogs to become the associate of man. A dog without a master is a forlorn creature; no society of other
dogs seems to console him; he wanders about disconsolate,
till he finds some human being to whom to attach himself,
and then he is a made dog,— he pads about with an air
of dignity, like a dog that is settled in life.

There are among dogs certain races or large divisions,
and those belonging purely to any of those races are called
blood-dogs. As examples of what we mean by these races,
we will mention the spaniel, the mastiff, the bulldog, the
hound, and the terrier; and each of these divisions contains

many species, and each has a strongly marked character. The spaniel tribes are gentle, docile, easily attached to man ; from them many hunting dogs are trained. The bulldog is irritable, a terrible fighter, and fiercely faithful to his master. A mastiff is strong, large, not so fierce as the bulldog, but watchful and courageous, with a peculiar sense of responsibility in guarding anything which is placed under his charge. The hounds are slender, lean, wiry, with a long, pointed muzzle, and a peculiar sensibility in the sense of smell, and their instincts lead them to hunting and tracking. As a general thing, they are cowardly and indisposed to combat; there are, however, remarkable exceptions, as you will see if you read the account of the good black hound which Sir Walter Scott tells about in " The Talisman," — a story which I advise you to read at your next leisure. The terriers are, for the most part, small dogs, smart, bright, and active, very intelligent, and capable of being taught many tricks. Of these there are several varieties, — as the English black and tan, which is the neatest and prettiest pet a family of children can have, as his hair is so short and close that he can harbor no fleas, and he is always good-tempered, lively, and affectionate. The Skye terrier, with his mouse-colored mop of hair, and his great bright eyes, is very loving and very sagacious ; but alas ! unless you can afford a great deal of time for soap, water, and fine-tooth-comb exercises, he will bring

more company than you will like.　The Scotch terriers
are rough, scraggy, affectionate, but so nervous, frisky, and
mischievous that they are only to be recommended as out-
door pets in barn and stable.　They are capital rat-catchers,
very amicable with horses, and will sit up by the driver or
a coach-boy with an air of great sagacity.

There is something very curious about the habits and
instincts of certain dogs which have been trained by man
for his own purposes.　In the mountains of Scotland, there
are a tribe of dogs called Shepherd-dogs, which for generations and ages have helped the shepherds to take care of
their sheep and which look for all the world like long-
nosed, high-cheek-boned, careful old Scotchmen.　You will
see them in the morning, trotting out their flock of sheep,
walking about with a grave, care-taking air, and at evening
all bustle and importance, hurrying and scurrying hither
and thither, getting their charge all together for the night.
An old Scotchman tells us that his dog Hector, by long
sharing his toils and cares, got to looking so much like
him, that once, when he felt too sleepy to go to meeting,
he sent Hector to take his seat in the pew, and the minister never knew the difference, but complimented him the
next day for his good attention to the sermon.

There is a kind of dog employed by the monks of St.
Bernard, in the Alps, to go out and seek in the snow for
travellers who may have lost their way; and this habit

becomes such a strong instinct in them, that I once knew a puppy of this species which was brought by a shipmaster to Maine, and grew up in a steady New England town, which used to alarm his kind friends by rushing off into the pine forest in snow-storms, and running anxiously up and down burrowing in the snow as if in quest of something.

I have seen one of a remarkable breed of dogs that are brought from the island of Manilla. They resemble mastiffs in their form, but are immensely large and strong. They are trained to detect thieves, and kept by merchants on board of vessels where the natives are very sly and much given to stealing. They are called *holders*, and their way is, when a strange man, whose purposes they do not understand, comes on board the ship, to take a very gentle but decisive hold of him by the heel, and keep him fast until somebody comes to look after him. The dog I knew of this species stood about as high as an ordinary dining-table, and I have seen him stroke off the dinner-cloth with one wag of his tail in his pleasure when I patted his head. He was very intelligent and affectionate.

There is another dog, which may often be seen in Paris, called the Spitz dog. He is a white, smooth-haired, small creature, with a great muff of stiff hair round his neck, and generally comes into Paris riding horseback on the cart-horses which draw the carts of the washerwomen. He races nimbly up and down on the back of the great heavy horses, barking from right to left with great animation, and is said to be a most faithful little creature in guarding the property of his owner. What is peculiar about these little dogs is the entireness of their devotion to their master They have not a look, not a wag of the tail, for any one else; it is vain for a stranger to try and make friends with them, — they have eyes and ears for one alone.

All dogs which do not belong to some of the great varieties, on the one side of their parentage or the other, are classed together as curs, and very much undervalued and decried; and yet among these mongrel curs we have seen individuals quite as sagacious, intelligent, and affectionate as the best blood-dogs.

And now I want to say some things to those young people who desire to adopt as domestic pets either a dog or a cat. Don't do it without making up your mind to be really and thoroughly kind to them, and feeding them as carefully as you feed yourself, and giving them appropriate shelter from the inclemency of the weather.

Some people seem to have a general idea that throwing a scrap, or bone, or bit of refuse meat, at odd intervals, to a dog, is taking abundant care of him. "What's the matter with him? he can't be hungry, — I gave him that great bone yesterday." Ah, Master Hopeful, how would you like to be fed on the same principle? When you show your hungry face at the dinner-table, suppose papa should say, "What's that boy here for? He was fed this morn ing." You would think this hard measure; yet a dog's oi cat's stomach digests as rapidly as yours. In like manner, dogs are often shut out of the house in cold winter weather without the least protection being furnished them. A lady and I looked out once, in a freezing icy day, and saw a great Newfoundland cowering in a corner of a fence to keep from the driving wind; and I said, "Do tell me if you have no kennel for that poor creature." "No," said the lady. "I didn't know that dogs needed shelter. Now I think of it, I remember last spring he seemed quite poorly, and his hair seemed to come out; do you suppose it was being exposed so much in the winter?" This lady had taken into her family a living creature, without ever having reflected on what that creature needed, or that it was her duty to provide for its wants.

Dogs can bear more cold than human beings, but they do not like cold any better than we do; and when a dog has his choice, he will very gladly stretch himself on a rug before the fire for his afternoon nap, and show that he enjoys the blaze and warmth as much as anybody.

As to cats, many people seem to think that a miserable, half-starved beast, never fed, and always hunted and beaten, and with no rights that anybody is bound to respect, is a necessary appendage to a family. They have the idea that

all a cat is good for is to catch rats, and that if well fed
they will not do this, — and so they starve them.   This is
a mistake in fact.   Cats are hunting animals, and have the
natural instinct to pursue and catch prey, and a cat that is
a good mouser will do this whether well or ill fed.   To live
only upon rats is said to injure the health of the cat, and
bring on convulsions.

The most beautiful and best trained cat I ever knew was
named Juno, and was brought up by a lady who was so
wise in all that related to the care and management of
animals, that she might be quoted as authority on all
points of their nurture and breeding ; and Juno, carefully
trained by such a mistress, was a standing example of the
virtues which may be formed in a cat by careful education.

Never was Juno known to be out of place, to take her
nap elsewhere than on her own appointed cushion, to be
absent at meal-times, or, when the most tempting dainties
were in her power, to anticipate the proper time by jumping on the table to help herself.

In all her personal habits Juno was of a neatness unpar-
alleled in cat history.   The parlor of her mistress was
always of a waxen and spotless cleanness, and Juno would
have died sooner than violate its sanctity by any impro-
priety.   She was a skilful mouser, and her sleek, glossy
sides were a sufficient refutation of the absurd notion that
a cat must be starved into a display of her accomplish·

ments. Every rat, mouse, or ground mole that she caught was brought in and laid at the feet of her mistress for approbation. But on one point her mind was dark. She could never be made to comprehend the great difference between fur and feathers, nor see why her mistress should gravely reprove her when she brought in a bird, and warmly commend when she captured a mouse.

After a while a little dog named Pero, with whom Juno had struck up a friendship, got into the habit of coming to her mistress's apartment at the hours when her modest meals were served, on which occasions Pero thought it would be a good idea to invite himself to make a third. He had a nice little trick of making himself amiable, by sitting up on his haunches, and making little begging gestures with his two fore-paws, — which so much pleased his hostess that sometimes he was fed before Juno. Juno observed this in silence for some time; but at last a bright idea struck her, and, gravely rearing up on her haunches, she imitated Pero's gestures with her fore-paws. Of course this carried the day, and secured her position.

Cats are often said to have no heart, — to be attached to places, but incapable of warm personal affection. It was reserved for Juno by her sad end to refute this slander on her race. Her mistress was obliged to leave her quiet home, and go to live in a neighboring city; so she gave Juno to the good lady who inhabited the other part of the house.

But no attentions or care on the part of her new mistress could banish from Juno's mind the friend she had lost.
The neat little parlor where she had spent so many pleasant
hours was dismantled and locked up, but Juno would go,
day after day, and sit on the ledge of the window-seat,
looking in and mewing dolefully. She refused food; and,
when too weak to mount on the sill and look in, stretched
herself on the ground beneath the window, where she died
for love of her mistress, as truly as any lover in an old
ballad.

You see by this story the moral that I wish to convey.
It is, that watchfulness, kindness, and care will develop a
nature in animals such as we little dream of. Love will
beget love, regular care and attention will give regular
habits, and thus domestic pets may be made agreeable and
interesting.

Any one who does not feel an inclination or capacity to
take the amount of care and pains necessary for the well-
being of an animal ought conscientiously to abstain from
having one in charge. A carefully tended pet, whether dog
or cat, is a pleasant addition to a family of young people;
but a neglected, ill-brought-up, ill-kept one is only an an-
noyance.

We should remember, too, in all our dealings with animals, that they are a sacred trust to us from our Heavenly
Father. They are dumb, and cannot speak for themselves;

they cannot explain their wants or justify their conduct; and therefore we should be tender towards them.

Our Lord says not even a little sparrow falls to the ground without our Heavenly Father, and we may believe that his eye takes heed of the disposition which we show towards those defenceless beings whom he thinks worthy of his protection.

AUNT ESTHER'S RULES.

IN the last number I told my little friends about my good Aunt Esther, and her wonderful cat Juno, and her dog Pero. In thinking what to write for this month, my mind goes far back to the days when I was a little girl, and used to spend many happy hours in Aunt Esther's parlor talking with her. Her favorite subject was always the habits and character of different animals, and their various ways and instincts, and she used to tell us so many wonderful, yet perfectly authentic, stories about all these things, that the hours passed away very quickly.

Some of her rules for the treatment and care of animals have impressed themselves so distinctly on my mind, that I shall never forget them, and I am going to repeat some of them to you.

One was, never to frighten an animal for sport. I recollect I had a little white kitten, of which I was very fond, and one day I was amusing myself with making her walk up and down the key-board of the piano, and laughing to see her fright at the strange noises which came up under her feet. Puss evidently thought the place was haunted, and tried to escape; it never occurred to me, however, that there was any cruelty in the operation, till Aunt Esther said to me, "My dear, you must never frighten an animal. I have suffered enough from fear to know that there is no suffering more dreadful; and a helpless animal, that cannot speak to tell its fright, and cannot understand an explanation of what alarms it, ought to move your pity."

I had never thought of this before, and then I remembered how, when I was a very, very little girl, a grown-up boy in school had amused himself with me and my little brother in much the same way as that in which I had amused myself with the kitten. He hunted us under one of the school-room tables by threatening to cut our ears off if we came out, and took out his pen-knife, and opened it, and shook it at us whenever we offered to move. Very likely he had not the least idea that we really could be made to suffer with fear at so absurd a threat, — any more than I had that my kitten could possibly be afraid of the piano; but our suffering was in fact as real as if the boy really had intended what he said, and was really able to execute it.

Another thing which Aunt Esther strongly impressed on my mind was, that, when there were domestic animals about a house which were not wanted in a family, it was far kinder to have them killed in some quick and certain way than to chase them out of the house, and leave them to wander homeless, to be starved, beaten, and abused.

Aunt Esther was a great advocate for killing animals, and, tender-hearted as she was, she gave us many instructions in the kindest and quickest way of disposing of one whose life must be sacrificed.

Her instructions sometimes bore most remarkable fruits. I recollect one little girl, who had been trained under Aunt Esther's care, was once coming home from school across Boston Common, when she saw a party of noisy boys and dogs tormenting a poor kitten by the side of the frog pond. The little wretches would throw it into the water, and then laugh at its vain and frightened efforts to paddle out, while the dogs added to its fright by their ferocious barking. Belle was a bright-eyed, spirited little puss, and her whole soul was roused in indignation; she dashed in among the throng of boys and dogs, and rescued the poor half-drowned little animal. The boys, ashamed, slunk away, and little Belle held the poor, cold, shivering little creature, considering what to do for it. It was half dead already, and she was embarrassed by the reflection that at home there was no room for another pet, for both cat and kitten never were wanting in their family. "Poor kit," she said, "you must die, but I will see that you are not tormented"; — and she knelt bravely down and held the little thing under water, with the tears running down her own cheeks, till all its earthly sorrows were over, and little kit was beyond the reach of dog or boy.

This was real brave humanity. Many people call themselves tender-hearted, because they are unwilling to have a
litter of kittens killed, and so they go and throw them
over fences, into people's back yards, and comfort themselves with the reflection that they will do well enough.
What becomes of the poor little defenceless things? In
nine cases out of ten they live a hunted, miserable life,
crying from hunger, shivering with cold, harassed by cruel
dogs, and tortured to make sport for brutal boys. How
much kinder and more really humane to take upon ourselves the momentary suffering of causing the death of an
animal than to turn our back and leave it to drag out
a life of torture and misery!

Aunt Esther used to protest much against another kind
of torture which well-meaning persons inflict on animals, in
giving them as playthings to very, little children who do
not know how to handle them. A mother sometimes will
sit quietly sewing, while her baby boy is tormenting a helpless kitten, poking his fingers into its eyes, pulling its tail,
stretching it out as on a rack, squeezing its feet, and, when
the poor little tormented thing tries to run away, will send
the nurse to catch dear little Johnny's kitten for him.

Aunt Esther always remonstrated, too, against all the
practical jokes and teasing of animals, which many people
practise under the name of sport, — like throwing a dog
into the water for the sake of seeing him paddle out, dash-

ing water upon the cat, or doing any of the many little
tricks by which animals are made uncomfortable. "They
have but one short little life to live, they are dumb and
cannot complain, and they are wholly in our powei"—
these were the motives by which she appealed to our generosity.

Aunt Esther's boys were so well trained, that they would
fight valiantly for the rescue of any ill-treated animals.
Little Master Bill was a bright-eyed fellow, who was n't
much taller than his father's knee, and wore a low-necked
dress with white ruffles. But Bill had a brave heart in his
little body, and so one day, as he was coming from school,
he dashed in among a crowd of dogs which were pursuing
a kitten, took it away from them, and held it as high above
his head as 'his little arm could reach. The dogs jumped
upon his white neck with their rough paws, and scratched
his face, but still he stood steady till a man came up and
took the kitten and frightened away the dogs. Master Bill
grew up to be a man, and at the battle of Gettysburg stood
a three days' fight, and resisted the charge of the Louisiana
Tigers as of old he withstood the charge of the dogs. A
really brave-hearted fellow is generally tender and compas-
sionate to the weak; only cowards torment that which is
not strong enough to fight them; only cowards starve helpless prisoners or torture helpless animals.

I can't help hoping that, in these stories about different

pets, I have made some friends among the boys, and that they will remember what I have said, and resolve always to defend the weak, and not permit any cruelty where it is in their power to prevent it. Boys, you are strong and brave little fellows; but you ought n't to be strong and brave for nothing; and if every boy about the street would set himself to defending helpless animals, we should see much less cruelty than we now do.

AUNT ESTHER'S STORIES.

AUNT ESTHER used to be a constant attendant upon us young ones whenever we were a little ill, or any of the numerous accidents of childhood overtook us. In such seasons of adversity she always came to sit by our bedside, and take care of us. She did not, as some people do, bring a long face and a doleful whining voice into a sick-room, but was always so bright, and cheerful, and chatty, that we began to think it was almost worth while to be sick to have her about us. I remember that once, when I had the quinsy, and my throat was so swollen that it brought the tears every time I swallowed, Aunt Esther talked to me so gayly, and told me so many stories, that I found myself laughing heartily, and disposed to regard my aching throat as on the whole rather an amusing circumstance.

Aunt Esther's stories were not generally fairy tales, but stories about real things, — and more often on her favorite subject of the habits of animals, and the different animals she had known, than about anything else.

One of these was a famous Newfoundland dog, named Prince, which belonged to an uncle of hers in the country, and was, as we thought, a far more useful and faithful member of society than many of us youngsters. Prince used to be a grave, sedate dog, that considered himself put in trust of the farm, the house, the cattle, and all that was on the place. At night he slept before the kitchen door, which, like all other doors in the house in those innocent days, was left unlocked all night ; and if such a thing had ever happened as that a tramper or an improper person of any kind had even touched the latch of the door, Prince would have been up attending to him as master of cere-monies.

At early dawn, when the family began to stir, Prince was up and out to superintend the milking of the cows, after which he gathered them all together, and started out with them to pasture, padding steadily along behind, dash-ing out once in a while to reclaim some wanderer that thoughtlessly began to make her breakfast by the roadside, instead of saving her appetite for the pastures, as a prop-erly behaved cow should. Arrived at the pasture-lot, Prince would take down the bars with his teeth, drive in the cows, put up bars, and then soberly turn tail and pad off home, and carry the dinner-basket for the men to the mowing lot, or the potato-field, or wherever the labors of the day might be. There arrived, he was extremely useful to send on errands after anything forgotten or missing. "Prince! the rake is missing: go to the barn and fetch it!" and away Prince would go, and come back with his

head very high, and the long rake very judiciously bal-
anced in his mouth.

One day a friend was wondering at the sagacity of the
dog, and his master thought he would show off his tricks
in a still more original style; and so, calling Prince to
him, he said, "Go home and bring Puss to me!"

Away bounded Prince towards the farm-house, and, looking about, found the younger of the two cats, fair Mistress
Daisy, busy cleaning her white velvet in the summer sun.
Prince took her gently up by the nape of her neck, and
carried her, hanging head and heels together, to the fields,
and laid her down at his master's feet.

"How 's this, Prince?" said the master; "you did n't
understand me. I said the cat, and this is the kitten.
Go right back and bring the old cat."

. Prince looked very much ashamed of his mistake, and
turned away, with drooping ears and tail, and went back
to the house.

The old cat was a venerable, somewhat portly old dame,
and no small lift for Prince; but he reappeared with old
Puss hanging from his jaws, and set her down, a little discomposed, but not a whit hurt by her unexpected ride.

Sometimes, to try Prince's skill, his master would hide
his gloves or riding-whip in some out-of-the-way corner,
and when ready to start, would say, "Now, where have I
left my gloves? Prince, good fellow, run in, and find

them"; and Prince would dash into the house, and run hither and thither with his nose to every nook and corner of the room; and, no matter how artfully they were hid, he would upset and tear his way to them. He would turn up the corners of the carpet, snuff about the bed, run his nose between the feather-bed and mattress, pry into the crack of a half-opened drawer, and show as much zeal and ingenuity as a policeman, and seldom could anything be so hid as to baffle his perseverance.

Many people laugh at the idea of being careful of a

dog's feelings, as if it were the height of absurdity; and yet it is a fact that some dogs are as exquisitely sensitive to pain, shame, and mortification, as any human being.   See, when a dog is spoken harshly to, what a universal droop seems to come over him.   His head and ears sink, his tail drops and slinks between his legs, and his whole air seems to say, "I wish I could sink into the earth to hide myself."

Prince's young master, without knowing it, was the means of inflicting a most terrible mortification on him at one time.   It was very hot weather, and Prince, being a shaggy dog, lay panting, and lolling his tongue out, apparently suffering from the heat.

"I declare," said young Master George, "I do believe Prince would be more comfortable for being sheared."   And so forthwith he took him and began divesting him of his coat.   Prince took it all very obediently; but when he appeared without his usual attire, every one saluted him with roars of laughter, and Prince was dreadfully mortified.   He broke away from his master, and scampered off home at a desperate pace, ran down cellar and disappeared from view. His young master was quite distressed that Prince took the matter so to heart; he followed him in vain, calling, "Prince! Prince!"   No Prince appeared.   He lighted a candle and searched the cellar, and found the poor creature cowering away in the darkest nook under the stairs. Prince was not to be comforted; he slunk deeper and

deeper into the darkness, and crouched on the ground
when he saw his master, and for a long time refused even
to take food. The family all visited and condoled with him,
and finally his sorrows were somewhat abated; but he
would not be persuaded to leave the cellar for nearly a
week. Perhaps by that time he indulged the hope that
his hair was beginning to grow again, and all were careful
not to destroy the allusion by any jests or comments on
his appearance.

Such were some of the stories of Prince's talents and
exploits which Aunt Esther used to relate to us. What
finally became of the old fellow we never heard. Let us
hope that, as he grew old, and gradually lost his strength,
and felt the infirmities of age creeping on, he was tenderly
and kindly cared for in memory of the services of his best
days, — that he had a warm corner by the kitchen fire,
and was daily spoken to in kindly tones by his old friends.
Nothing is a sadder sight than to see a poor old favorite,
that once was petted and caressed by every member of
the family, now sneaking and cowering as if dreading
every moment a kick or a blow, — turned from the parlor
into the kitchen, driven from the kitchen by the cook's
broomstick, half starved and lonesome.

O, how much kinder if the poor thread of life were at
once cut by some pistol-shot, than to have the neglected
favorite linger only to suffer! Now, boys, I put it to you.

is it generous or manly, when your old pet and - .ate grows sickly and feeble, and can no longer amuse you, to forget all the good old times you have had with him, and let him become a poor, trembling, hungry, abused vagrant? If you cannot provide comforts for his old age, and see to his nursing, you can at least secure him an easy and painless passage from this troublesome world. A manly fellow I once knew, who, when his old hound became so diseased that he only lived to suffer, gave him a nice meal with his own hand, patted his head, got him to sleep, and then shot him, — so that he was dead in a moment, felt no pain, and knew nothing but kindness to the last.

And now to Aunt Esther's stories of a dog I must add one more which occurred in a town where I once lived. I have told you of the fine traits of blood-dogs, their sagacity and affection. In doing this, perhaps, I have not done half justice to the poor common dogs, of no particular blood or breed, that are called curs or mongrels; yet among these I believe you will quite as often find both affection and sagacity as among better-born dogs.

The poor mongrel I am going to tell you about belonged to a man who had not, in one respect, half the sense that his dog had. A dog will never eat or drink a thing that has once made him sick, or injured him; but this man would drink, time and time again, a deadly draught, that took away his senses and unfitted him for any of his duties.

Poor little Pero, however, set her ignorant dog's heart on her drinking master, and used to patter faithfully after him, and lick his hand respectfully, when nobody else thought he was in a condition to be treated with respect.

One bitter cold winter day, Pero's master went to a grocery, at some distance from home, on pretence of getting groceries, but in reality to fill a very dreadful bottle, that was the cause of all his misery; and little Pero padded after him through the whirling snow, although she left three poor little pups of her own in the barn. Was it that she was anxious for the poor man who was going the bad road, or was there some secret thing in her dog's heart that warned her that her master was in danger? We know not, but the sad fact is, that at the grocery the poor man took enough to make his brain dizzy, and coming home he lost his way in a whirling snow-storm, and fell down stupid and drunk, not far from his own barn, in a lonesome place, with the cold winter's wind sweeping the snow-drift over him. Poor little Pero cuddled close to her master and nestled in his bosom, as if trying to keep the warm life in him.

Two or three days passed, and nothing was seen or heard of the poor man. The snow had drifted over him in a long white winding-sheet, when a neighbor one day heard a dog in the barn crying to get out. It was poor Pero, that had come back and slipped in to nurse her

puppies while the barn-door was open, and was now crying
to get out and go back to her poor master. It suddenly
occurred to the man that Pero might find the body, and
in fact, when she started off, he saw a little path which
her small paws had worn in the snow, and, tracking after,
found the frozen body. This poor little friend had nestled
the snow away around the breast, and stayed watching
and waiting by her dead master, only taking her way
back occasionally to the barn to nurse her little ones. I
cannot help asking whether a little animal that can show
such love and faithfulness has not something worth respect-
ing and caring for in its nature.

At this time of the year our city ordinances proclaim
a general leave and license to take the lives of all dogs
found in the streets, and scenes of dreadful cruelty are
often enacted in consequence. I hope, if my stories fall
under the eye of any boy who may ever witness, or be
tempted to take part in, the hunting down and killing a
poor dog, that he will remember of how much faithfulness
and affection and constancy these poor brutes are capable,
and, instead of being their tyrant and persecutor, will try
to make himself their protector and friend.

SIR WALTER SCOTT AND HIS DOGS.

MASTER Frederick Little-John has of late struck up quite a friendship with me, and haunts my footsteps about house to remind me of my promise to write some more dog stories. Master Fred has just received a present from his father of a great Newfoundland that stands a good deal higher in his stocking-feet than his little master in his highest-heeled boots, and he has named him Prince, in honor of the Prince that I told you about last month, that used to drive the cows to pasture, and take down the bars with his teeth. We have daily and hourly accounts in the family circle of Prince's sayings and doings; for Master Freddy insists upon it that Prince speaks, and daily insists upon placing a piece of bread on the top of Prince's nose, which at the word of command he fires into the air, and catches in his mouth, closing the performance with a snap like a rifle. Fred also makes much of showing him a bit of meat held high in the air, from which he is requested to "speak," — the speaking consisting in very short exclamations of the deepest bow-wow. Certain it is that Prince shows on these occasions that he has the voice for a public speaker, and that, if he does not go about the country lecturing, it is because he wants time yet to make up his mind what to say on the topics of the day.

Fred is somewhat puzzled to make good the ground of his favorite with Aunt Zeroiah, who does not love dogs, and is constantly casting reflections on them as nuisances, dirt-makers, flea-catchers, and flea-scatterers, and insinuating a plea that Prince should be given away, or in some manner sold or otherwise disposed of.

"Aunt Zeroiah thinks that there is nothing so mean as a dog," said Master Fred to me as he sat with his arm around the neck of his favorite. "She really seems to grudge every morsel of meat a dog eats, and to think that every kindness you show a dog is almost a sin. Now I think dogs are noble creatures, and have noble feelings, —they are so faithful, and so kind and loving. Now I do wish you would make haste and write something to show her that dogs have been thought a good deal of."

"Well, Master Freddy," said I, "I will tell you in the first place about Sir Walter Scott, whose poems and novels have been the delight of whole generations."

He was just of your opinion about dogs, and he had a great many of them. When Washington Irving visited Sir Walter at Abbotsford, he found him surrounded by his dogs, which formed as much a part of the family as his children.

In the morning, when they started for a ramble, the

dogs would all be on the alert to join them. There was first a tall old staghound named Maida, that considered himself the confidential friend of his master, walked by his side, and looked into his eyes as if asserting a partnership in his thoughts. Then there was a black greyhound named Hamlet, a more frisky and thoughtless youth, that gambolled and pranced and barked and cut capers with the wildest glee ; and there was a beautiful setter

named Finette, with large mild eyes, soft silken hair, and long curly ears, — the favorite of the parlor ; and then a venerable old greyhound, wagging his tail, came out to join the party as he saw them going by his quarters, and was cheered by Scott with a hearty, kind word as an old friend and comrade.

In his walks Scott would often stop and talk to one or another of his four-footed friends, as if they were in fact rational companions ; and, from being talked to and treated in this way, they really seemed to acquire more sagacity than other dogs.

Old Maida seemed to consider himself as a sort of president of the younger dogs, as a dog of years and reflection, whose mind was upon more serious and weighty topics than theirs. As he padded along, the younger dogs would sometimes try to ensnare him into a frolic, by jumping upon his neck and making a snap at his ears. Old Maida would bear this in silent dignity for a while, and then suddenly, as if his patience were exhausted, he would catch one of his tormentors by the neck and tumble him in the dirt, giving an apologetic look to his master at the same time, as much as to say, " You see, sir, I can't help joining a little in this nonsense."

" Ah," said Scott, " I 've no doubt that, when Maida is alone with these young dogs, he throws dignity aside and plays the boy as much as any of them, but he is ashamed to do it in our company, and seems to say, 'Have done with your nonsense, youngsters; what will the Laird and that other gentleman think of me if I give way to such foolery?'"

At length the younger dogs fancied that they discovered something, which set them all into a furious barking. Old Maida for some time walked silently by his master, pretending not to notice the clamors of the inferior dogs. At last, however, he seemed to feel himself called on to attend to them, and giving a plunge forward he opened his mind to them with a deep "Bow-wow," that drowned for the time all other noises. Then, as if he had settled matters, he returned to his master, wagging his tail, and looking in his face as if for approval.

"Ay, ay, old boy," said Scott; "you have done wonders; you have shaken the Eildon Hills with your roaring, and now you may shut up your artillery for the rest of the day. Maida," he said, "is like the big gun of Constantinople, — it takes so long to get it ready that the small ones can fire off a dozen times, but when it does go off it carries all before it."

Scott's four-footed friends made a respectful part of the company at family meals. Old Maida took his seat gravely at his master's elbow, looking up wistfully into his eyes, while Finette, the pet spaniel, took her seat by Mrs. Scott. Besides the dogs in attendance, a large gray cat also took

her seat near her master, and was presented from time to
time with bits from the table.   Puss, it appears, was a
great favorite both with master and mistress, and slept in
their room at night; and Scott laughingly said that one
of the least wise parts of the family arrangement was the
leaving the window open at night for puss to go in and
out.   The cat assumed a sort of supremacy among the
quadrupeds, sitting in state in Scott's arm-chair, and occasionally stationing himself on a chair beside the door, as
if to review his subjects as they passed, giving each dog
a cuff on the ears as he went by.   This clapper-clawing
was always amiably taken.   It appeared to be in fact a
mere act of sovereignty on the part of Grimalkin, to remind
the others of their vassalage, to which they cheerfully submitted.   Perfect harmony prevailed between old puss and
her subjects, and they would all sleep contentedly together
in the sunshine.

Scott once said, the only trouble about having a dog
was that he must die; but he said, it was better to have
them die in eight or nine years, than to go on loving
them for twenty or thirty, and then have them die.

Scott lived to lose many of his favorites, that were
buried with funeral honors, and had monuments erected
over them, which form some of the prettiest ornaments of
Abbotsford.   When we visited the place, one of the first
objects we saw in the front yard near the door was the

tomb of old Maida, over which is sculptured the image of
a beautiful hound, with this inscription, which you may
translate if you like : —

> "Maidae marmorea dormis, sub imagine
> Maida,
> Ad januam domini ; sit tibi terra levis.

Or, if you don't want the trouble of translating it, Master Freddy, I would do it thus : —

> "At thy lord's door, in slumbers light and blest,
> Maida, beneath this marble Maida rest.
> Light lie the turf upon thy gentle breast."

Washington Irving says that in one of his morning
rambles he came upon a curious old Gothic monument,
on which was inscribed in Gothic characters,

> "Cy git le preux Percy,"
> (Here lies the brave Percy,)

and asking Scott what it was, he replied, "O, only one of
my fooleries," — and afterwards Irving found it was the
grave of a favorite greyhound.

Now, certainly, Master Freddy, you must see in all this
that you have one of the greatest geniuses of the world to
bear you out in thinking a deal of dogs.

But I have still another instance. The great rival poet
to Scott was Lord Byron ; not so good or so wise a man
by many degrees, but very celebrated in his day. He also

had a four-footed friend, a Newfoundland, called Boatswain, which he loved tenderly, and whose elegant monument now forms one of the principal ornaments of the garden of Newstead Abbey, and upon it may be read this inscription : —

> " Near this spot
> Are deposited the remains of one
> Who possessed beauty without vanity,
> Strength without insolence,
> Courage without ferocity,
> And all the virtues of man without his vices.
> This praise, which would be unmeaning flattery
> If inscribed over human ashes,
> Is but a just tribute to the memory of
> BOATSWAIN, a dog,
> Who was born at Newfoundland, May, 1803,
> And died at Newstead Abbey, Nov. 18, 1808."

On the other side of the monument the poet inscribed these lines in praise of dogs in general, which I would recommend you to show to any of the despisers of dogs:—

> " When some proud son of man returns to earth
> Unknown to glory, but upheld by birth,
> The sculptor's art exhausts the pomp of woe,
> And storied urns record who rests below.
> But the poor dog, in life the firmest friend,
> The first to welcome, foremost to defend,
> Whose honest heart is still his master's own,
> Who labors, fights, lives, breathes, for him alone,
> Unhonored falls, unnoticed all his worth,
> Denied in heaven the soul he held on earth.

> While man, vain insect! hopes to be forgiven,
> And claims himself a sole exclusive heaven!
> Ye who perchance behold this simple urn,
> Pass on, it honors none you wish to mourn.
> To mark a *friend's* remains these stones arise;
> I never knew but one, — and here he lies."

If you want more evidence of the high esteem in which dogs are held, I might recommend to you a very pretty dog story called "Rab and his Friends," the reading of which will give you a pleasant hour. Also in a book called "Spare Hours," the author of "Rab and his Friends" gives amusing accounts of all his different dogs, which I am sure you would be pleased to read, even though you find many long words in it which you cannot understand.

But enough has been given to show you that in the high esteem you have for your favorite, and in your determination to treat him as a dog should be treated, you are sustained by the very best authority.

COUNTRY NEIGHBORS AGAIN

DO my dear little friends want to hear a word more about our country neighbors? Since we wrote about them, we have lived in the same place more than a year, and perhaps some of you may want to know whether old Unke or little Cri-cri have ever come up to sit under the lily-leaves by the fountain, or 'Master Furry-toes, the flying squirrel, has amused himself in pattering about the young lady's chamber o' nights? I am sorry to say that our country neighbors have entirely lost the neighborly, confiding spirit that they had when we first came and settled in the woods.

Old Unke has distinguished himself on moonlight nights in performing bass solos in a very deep, heavy voice, down in the river, but he has never hopped his way back into that conservatory from which he was disgracefully turned out at the point of Mr. Fred's cane. He has contented himself with the heavy musical performances I spoke of, and I have fancied they sounded much like "Won't come any more, — won't come any more, — won't come any more!"

Sometimes, strolling down to the river, we have seen his solemn green spectacles emerging from the tall water-grasses, as he sat complacently looking about him. Near by him, spread out on the sunny bottom of the pool, was a large flat-headed water-snake, with a dull yellow-brown back and such a swelled stomach that it was quite evident he had been making his breakfast that morning by swallowing some unfortunate neighbor like poor little Cri-cri. This trick of swallowing one's lesser neighbors seems to prevail greatly among the people who live in our river. Mr. Water-snake makes his meal on little Mr. Frog, and Mr. Bullfrog follows the same example. It seems a sad state of things : but then I suppose all animals have to die in some way or other, and perhaps, if they are in the habit of seeing it done, it may appear no more to a frog to expect to be swallowed some day, than it may to some of us to die of a fever, or be shot in battle, as many a brave fellow has been of late.

12

We have heard not a word from the woodchucks. Ever since we violated the laws of woodland hospitality by setting a trap for their poor old patriarch, they have very justly considered us as bad neighbors, and their hole at the bottom of the garden has been "to let," and nobody as yet has ventured to take it. Our friends the muskrats have been flourishing, and on moonlight nights have been swimming about, popping up the tips of their little black noses to make observations.

But latterly a great commotion has been made among the amphibious tribes, because of the letting down of the dam which kept up the water of the river, and made it a good, full, wide river. When the dam was torn down it became a little miserable stream, flowing through a wide field of muddy bottom, and all the secrets of the under-water were disclosed. The white and yellow water-lily roots were left high and dry up in the mud, and all the musk-rat holes could be seen plainer than ever before; and the other day Master Charlie brought in a fish's nest which he had found in what used to be deep water.

"A fish's nest!" says little Tom; "I did n't know fishes made nests." But they do, Tommy; that is, one particular kind of fish makes a nest of sticks and straws and twigs, plastered together with some kind of cement, the making of which is a family secret. It lies on the ground like a common bird's-nest turned bottom upward, and has a tiny

little hole in the side for a door, through which the little fishes swim in and out.

The name of the kind of fish that builds this nest I do not know; and if the water had not been drawn off, I should not have known that we had any such fish in our river. Where we found ours the water had been about

five feet above it.   Now, Master Tom, if you want to
know more about nest-building fishes, you must get your
papa and mamma to inquire and see if they cannot get
you some of the little books on fishes and aquariums that
have been published lately.   I remember to have read all
about these nests in one of them, but I do not remember
either the name of the book or the name of the fish, and
so there is something still for you to inquire after.

I am happy to say, for the interest of the water-lilies
and the muskrats and the fishes, that the dam has only
been torn down from our river for the purpose of making
a new and stronger one, and that by and by the water
will be again broad and deep as before, and all the water-
people can then go on with their housekeeping just as
they used to do, — only I am sorry to say that one fish
family will miss their house, and have to build a new one ;
but if they are enterprising fishes they will perhaps make
some improvements that will make the new house better
than the old.

As to the birds, we have had a great many visits from
them.   Our house has so many great glass windows, and
the conservatory windows in the centre of it being always
wide open, the birds seem to have taken it for a piece of
out-doors, and flown in.   The difficulty has been, that,
after they had got in, there appeared to be no way of
mak'ng them understand the nature of glass, and wher-

ever they saw a glass window they fancied they could fly
through ; and so, taking aim hither and thither, they darted
head first against the glass, beating and bruising their
poor little heads without beating in any more knowledge
than they had before. Many a poor little feather-head
has thus fallen a victim to his want of natural philosophy,
and tired himself out with beating against window-panes,
till he has at last fallen dead. One day we picked up no
less than three dead birds in different parts of the house.
Now if it had only been possible to enlighten our feathered
friends in regard to the fact that everything that is trans-
parent is not air, we would have summoned a bird council
in our conservatory, and explained matters to them at once
and altogether. As it is, we could only say, "Oh!" and
"Ah!" and lament, as we have followed one poor victim
after another from window to window, and seen him
flutter and beat his pretty senseless head against the glass,
frightened to death at all our attempts to help him.

As to the humming-birds, their number has been infinite.
Just back of the conservatory stands an immense, high
clump of scarlet sage, whose brilliant flowers have been
like a light shining from afar, and drawn to it flocks of
these little creatures ; and we have often sat watching them
as they put their long bills into one scarlet tube after
another, lifting themselves lightly off the bush, poising a
moment in mid-air, and then dropping out of sight.

They have flown into the conservatory in such nnmbers that, had we wished to act over again the dear little history of our lost pet, Hum, the son of Buz, we should have had plenty of opportunities to do it. Humming-birds have been for some reason supposed to be peculiarly wild and untamable. Our experience has proved that they are the most docile, confiding little creatures, and the most disposed to put trust in us human beings of all birds in the world.

More than once this summer has some little captive exhausted his strength flying hither and thither against the great roof window of the conservatory, till the whole family was in alarm to help. The Professor himself has left his books, and anxiously flourished a long cobweb broom in hopes to bring the little wanderer down to the level of open windows, while every other member of the family ran, called, made suggestions, and gave advice, which all ended in the poor little fool's falling flat, in a state of utter exhaustion, and being picked up in some lady's pocket-handkerchief.

Then has been running to mix sugar and water, while the little crumb of a bird has lain in an apparent swoon in the small palm of some fair hand, but opening occasionally one eye, and then the other, dreamily, to see when the sugar and water was coming, and gradually showing more and more signs of returning life as it appeared.

Even when he had taken his drink of sugar and water, and seemed able to sit up in his warm little hollow, he has seemed in no hurry to flee, but remained tranquilly looking about him for some moments, till all of a sudden, with one whirr, away he goes, like a flying morsel of green and gold, over our heads — into the air — into the tree-tops. What a lovely time he must have of it!

One rainy, windy day, Miss Jenny, going into the conservatory, heard a plaintive little squeak, and found a poor humming-bird, just as we found poor little Hum, all wet and chilled, and bemoaning himself, as he sat clinging tightly upon the slenderest twig of a grape-vine. She took him off, wrapped him in cotton, and put him in a box on a warm shelf over the kitchen range. After a while you may be sure there was a pretty fluttering in the box. Master Hum was awake and wanted to be attended to. She then mixed sugar and water, and, opening the box, offered him a drop on her finger, which he licked off with his long tongue as knowingly as did his namesake at Rye Beach. After letting him satisfy his appetite for sugar and water, as the rain was over and the sun began to shine, Miss Jenny took him to the door, and away he flew.

These little incidents show that it would not ever be a difficult matter to tame humming-birds, — only they cannot be kept in cages; a sunny room with windows defended by mosquito-netting would be the only proper cage. The humming-bird, as we are told by naturalists, though very fond of the honey of flowers, does not live on it entirely, or even principally. It is in fact a little fly-catcher, and lives on small insects; and a humming-bird never can be kept healthy for any length of time in a room that does not admit insects enough to furnish him a living. So you see it is not merely toads, and water-snakes, and such homely creatures, that live by eating other living beings, — but even the fairy-like and brilliant humming-bird.

The autumn months are now coming on (for it is October while I write), — the flowers are dying night by night as the frosts grow heavier, — the squirrels are racing about, full of business, getting in their winter's supply of nuts; everything now is active and busy among our country neighbors. In a cottage about a quarter of a mile from us, a whole family of squirrels have made the discovery that a house is warmer in winter than the best hollow tree, and so have gone in to a chink between the walls, where Mr. and Mrs. Squirrel can often be heard late at night chattering and making quite a family fuss about the arrangement of their household goods for the coming season. This is all the news about the furry people that I have to give you. The flying squirrel I have not yet heard from, — perhaps he will appear yet as the weather gets colder.

Old Master Boohoo, the owl, sometimes goes on at such a rate on moonlight nights in the great chestnut-trees that overhang the river, that, if you did not know better, you might think yourself miles deep in the heart of a sombre forest, instead of being within two squares' walk of the city lamps. We never yet have caught a fair sight of him. At the cottage we speak of, the chestnut-trees are very tall, and come close to the upper windows; and one night a fair maiden, going up to bed, was startled by a pair of great round eyes looking into her window. It was one of the Boohoo family, who had been taken with a fit. of grave curiosity about what went on inside the cottage, and so set himself to observe. We have never been able to return the compliment by looking into their housekeeping, as their nests are very high up in the hollows of old trees, where we should not be likely to get at them.

If we hear anything more from any of these neighbors of ours, we will let you know. We have all the afternoon been hearing a great screaming among the jays in the woods hard by, and I think we must go out and see what is the matter. So good by.

THE DIVERTING HISTORY OF LITTLE WHISKEY.

AND now, at the last, I am going to tell you something of the ways and doings of one of the queer little people, whom I shall call Whiskey.

On this page is his picture. But you cannot imagine from this how pretty he is. His back has the most beautiful smooth shining stripes of reddish brown and black, his eyes shine like bright glass beads, and he sits up jauntily on his hind quarters, with his little tail thrown over his back like a ruffle!

And where does he live? Well, "that is telling," as we

children say. It was somewhere up in the mountains of Berkshire, in a queer, quaint, old-fashioned garden, that I made Mr. Whiskey's acquaintance.

Here there lives a young parson, who preaches every Sunday in a little brown church, and during week-days goes through all these hills and valleys, visiting the poor, and gathering children into Sunday schools.

His wife is a very small-sized lady, — not much bigger than you, my little Mary, — but very fond of all sorts of dumb animals; and by constantly watching their actions and ways, she has come to have quite a strange power over them, as I shall relate.

The little lady fixed her mind on Whiskey, and gave him his name without consulting him upon the subject. She admired his bright eyes, and resolved to cultivate his acquaintance.

By constant watching, she discovered that he had a small hole of his own in the grass-plot a few paces from her back door. So she used to fill her pockets with hazelnuts, and go out and sit in the back porch, and make a little noise, such as squirrels make to each other, to attract his attention.

In a minute or two up would pop the little head with the bright eyes, in the grass-plot, and Master Whiskey would sit on his haunches and listen, with one small ear cocked towards her. Then she would throw him a hazelnut, and he would slip instantly down into his hole again. In a minute or two, however, his curiosity would get the better of his prudence; and she, sitting quiet, would see the little brown-striped head slowly, slowly coming up again, over the tiny green spikes of the grass-plot. Quick as a flash he would dart at the nut, whisk it into a little bag on one side of his jaws, which Madame Nature has furnished him with for his provision-pouch, and down into his hole again! An ungrateful, suspicious little brute he was too; for though in this way he bagged and carried off nut after nut, until the patient little woman had used up a pound of hazelnuts, still he seemed to have the same wild fright at sight of her, and would whisk off and hide himself in his hole the moment she appeared. In vain she called, "Whiskey, Whiskey, Whiskey," in the most flattering tones; in vain she coaxed and cajoled. No, no; he was not to be caught napping. He had no objection to accepting her nuts, as many as she chose to throw to him; but as to her taking any personal liberty with him, you see, it was not to be thought of!

But at last patience and perseverance began to have their reward. Little Master Whiskey said to himself, "Surely, this is a nice, kind lady, to take so much pains to give me nuts; she is certainly very considerate;" and with that he edged a little nearer and nearer every day, until, quite to the delight of the small lady, he would come and climb into her lap and seize the nuts, when she rattled them there, and after that he seemed to make exploring voyages all over her person. He would climb up and sit on her shoulder; he would mount and perch himself on her head; and, when she held a nut for him between her teeth, would take it out of her mouth.

After a while he began to make tours of discovery in the house. He would suddenly appear on the minister's writing-table, when he was composing his Sunday sermon, and sit cocking his little pert head at him, seeming to wonder what he was about. But in all his explorations he proved himself a true Yankee squirrel, having always a shrewd eye on the main chance. If the parson dropped a nut on the floor, down went Whiskey after it, and into his provision-bag it went, and then he would look up as if he expected another; for he had a wallet on each side of his jaws, and he always wanted both sides handsomely filled before he made for his hole. So busy and active, and always intent on this one object, was he, that before long the little lady found he had made way with six pounds of hazelnuts. His general rule was to carry off four nuts at a time, — three being stuffed into the side-pockets of his jaws, and the fourth held in his teeth. When he had furnished himself in this way, he would dart like lightning for his hole, and disappear in a moment; but in a short time up he would come, brisk and wide-awake, and ready for the next supply.

Once a person who had the curiosity to dig open a chipping squirrel's hole found in it two quarts of buckwheat, a quantity of grass-seed, nearly a peck of acorns, some Indian corn, and a quart of walnuts; a pretty handsome supply for a squirrel's winter store-room, — don't you think so?

Whiskey learned in time to work for his living in many artful ways that his young mistress devised. Sometimes she would tie his nuts up in a paper package, which he would attack with great energy, gnawing the strings, and rustling the nuts out of the paper in wonderfully quick time. Sometimes she would tie a nut to the end of a bit of twine, and swing it backward and forward over his head; and, after a succession of spry jumps, he would pounce upon it, and hang swinging on the twine, till he had gnawed the nut away.

Another squirrel — doubtless hearing of Whiskey's good luck — began to haunt the same yard; but Whiskey would by no means allow him to cultivate his young mistress's acquaintance. No indeed! he evidently considered that the institution would not support two. Sometimes he would appear to be conversing with the stranger on the most familiar and amicable terms in the back yard: but if his mistress called his name, he would immediately start and chase his companion quite out of sight, before he came back to her.

So you see that self-seeking is not confined to men alone, and that Whiskey's fine little fur coat covers a very selfish heart.

As winter comes on, Whiskey will go down into his hole, which has many long galleries and winding passages, and a snug little bedroom well lined with leaves. Here he will doze and dream away his long winter months, and nibble out the inside of his store of nuts.

If I hear any more of his cunning tricks, I will tell you of them.